FALCONI SHOUTED, "HERE THEY COME!"

And suddenly the jungle in front of the Black Eagles exploded with AK47 rounds and the shouts of command in Vietnamese.

Gunnar the Gunner saw his chance to contribute. His big M60 chugged away at one hundred rounds of sustained fire, the metal links of the ammo belts clinking and pinging as they bounced away from the weapon. The Black Eagles farther forward instinctively ducked their heads as Gunnar's rounds slapped the air inches above them. They spotted a team of NVA coming in from the side, but before they could respond Gunnar's fusillades shifted and sent green-uniformed enemy soldiers tumbling to the ground in bloody piles.

Falconi nodded his encouragement as he spoke into the Prick-Six. "Team leaders!" he yelled over the din. "Get those goddamn grenadiers to work!"

In moments the grenades began exploding in the Reds' midst for a full ten minutes of Black Eagle hell!

#13

ENCORE AT DIEN BIEN PHU

BLACK EAGLES

BY JOHN LANSING

ZEBRA BOOKS
KENSINGTON PUBLISHING CORP.

Special Acknowledgment to Patrick E. Andrews

ZEBRA BOOKS

are published by

Kensington Publishing Corp.
475 Park Avenue South
New York, NY 10016

First printing: October 1987

Printed in the United States of America

Dedicated to
CORPORAL WHEATFALL
of the 187th Airborne Regimental Combat Team
"The Rakkasans!"
And all the guys who trained on the 105s
at Fort Bragg in Area 7 back in 1955.

THE BLACK EAGLES ROLE OF HONOR

(Assigned or Attached Personnel Killed in Action)

Sgt. Barker, Toby — U.S. Marine Corps
Sgt. Barthe, Eddie — U.S. Army
Sgt. Bernstein, Jacob — U.S. Marine Corps
1st Lt. Blum, Marc — U.S. Air Force
Sgt. Boudreau, Marcel — U.S. Army
Chief Petty Officer Brewster, Leland — U.S. Navy
Sgt. Carter, Demond — U.S. Army
Master Sgt. Chun, Kim — South Korean Marines
Staff Sgt. Dayton, Marvin — U.S. Army
Sfc. Galchaser, Jack — U.S. Army
Lt. Hawkins, Chris — U.S. Navy
Sgt. Hodges, Trent — U.S. Army
Mr. Hosteins, Bruno — ex-French Foreign Legion
Petty Officer 2nd Class Jackson, Fred — U.S. Navy
Chief Petty Officer Jenkins, Claud — U.S. Navy
Spec. 4 Laird, Douglas — U.S. Army
Sgt. Limo, Raymond — U.S. Army
Petty Officer 3rd Class Littleton, Michael — U.S. Navy
Lt. Martin, Buzz — U.S. Navy
Petty Officer 2d Class Martin, Durwood — U.S. Navy
Sgt. Matsamura, Frank — U.S. Army
Staff Sgt. Maywood, Dennis — U.S. Army
Sfc. Miskoski, Jan — U.S. Army
Staff Sgt. Newcomb, Thomas — Australian Army
1st Lt. Nguyen Van Dow — South Vietnamese Army
Staff Sgt. O'Quinn, Liam — U.S. Marine Corps
Sfc. Ormond, Norman — U.S. Army
Sgt. Park, Chun Ri — South Korean Marines
Sfc. Rivera, Manuel — U.S. Army
Master Sgt. Snow, John — U.S. Army
Staff Sgt. Taylor, William — Australian Army

Lt. Thompson, William — U.S. Navy
Staff Sgt. Tripper, Charles — U.S. Army
1st Lt. Wakely, Richard — U.S. Army
Staff Sgt. Whitaker, George — Australian Army
Gunnery Sgt. White, Jackson — U.S. Marine Corps

ROSTER OF THE BLACK EAGLES
COMMAND ELEMENT

Lt. Col. Robert Falconi
U.S. Army
Commanding Officer
(13th Black Eagle Mission)

Petty Officer 1st Class Sparks Johnson
U.S. Navy
Communications Chief
(1st Black Eagle Mission

Sgt. Gunnar Olson
U.S. Army
Machine Gunner
(1st Black Eagle Mission)

Spec. 4 Tiny Burke
U.S. Army
Ammo Bearer
(1st Black Eagle Mission)

RAY'S ROUGHNECKS

2nd Lt. Ray Swift Elk
U.S. Army
Team Leader/Executive Officer
(11th Black Eagle Mission)

Staff Sgt. Paulo Garcia
U.S. Marine Corps
Auto Rifleman/Intelligence
(3rd Black Eagle Mission)

Sgt. Dwayne Simpson
U.S. Army
Grenadier
(2nd Black Eagle Mission)

Sgt. Jessie Maklue
U.S. Army
Rifleman
(1st Black Eagle Mission)

TOP'S TERRORS

Sgt. Major Top Gordon
U.S. Army
Team Leader/Detachment Sergeant
(10th Black Eagle Mission)

Sfc. Malcomb McCorckel
U.S. Army
Auto Rifleman/Medic
(11th Black Eagle Mission)

Staff Sgt. Salty O'Rourke
U.S. Marine Corps
Grenadier
(1st Black Eagle Mission)

Petty Officer 3rd Class Blue Richards
U.S. Navy

Rifleman/Demolitions
(6th Black Eagle Mission)

CALVIN'S CRAPSHOOTERS

Sfc. Calvin Culpepper
U.S. Army
Team Leader
(11th Black Eagle Mission)

Staff Sgt. Enrique Valverde
U.S. Army
Auto Rifleman/Supply
(4th Black Eagle Mission)

Petty Officer 3rd Class Richard Robichaux
U.S. Navy
Grenadier/Medic
(2nd Black Eagle Mission)

Sgt. Dean Fotopoulus
U.S. Army
Rifleman
(1st Black Eagle Mission)

A.W.O.L.

Sgt. Archie Dobbs
U.S. Army
(10 Black Eagle Mission)

Prologue

The Satellite Communications Control Station situated outside San Diego, California, hummed along in its quiet, low-keyed routine.

Deep inside the complex, in one of the monitoring stations, the control consoles were manned by highly trained technicians. The screens of these instruments gave every indication that the orbiting spheres of electronic communications equipment were operating as designed while the satellites they tracked circled the globe.

One of the technicians, assigned to a specific project designated by the acronym SCARS—Special Communication and Reporting Satellite—lazily sipped coffee and watched the cathode ray tube continue to display its comforting pattern of uninterrupted impulses across its green expanse.

Then it stopped.

The man, unconcerned, reached out with his free hand and gently pushed the RESET key.

Nothing happened.

He tried again. "Oh, hell!" he swore softly. He attempted to reset several more times without success. Finally, exasperated, he did a mini-boot, but still could get no results. Now angry and a bit frustrated, he brought the system down and took it through the complicated steps of a full boot.

Still with no results.

"Charlie!"

The senior engineer came over and was appraised of the situation. "Godamnit! You know SCARS isn't supposed to be out of monitor for more than five minutes."

"It won't take a boot," the technician complained.

The senior engineer, pressed a bit for time, tried a mini-boot also, but it wouldn't take. Rather than expend more valuable minutes, he went to the systems control room and tried a full boot from the computer programming unit.

There were absolutely no positive results.

"Harry!"

The chief engineer was brought onto the scene. He went to the back of the CPU and opened it up to expose the emergency system backup. He went through his assigned auxiliary routine with no success. Now sweating out a good ass-chewing since SCARS had been unmonitored for nine minutes, the chief went into full emergency procedures. This involved going into the center's vault and performing an electronic operation that some thought would bring dead people back to life.

But the SCARS screen remained blank.

The senior engineer looked up when the chief engineer came back from the vault. "Now what do we do?"

"There's only one guy to call," the chief said.

The senior nodded. "Yeah. Erickson."

"That's the guy that designed this baby," the technician said. He knew things were serious by then. "Where do you find him?"

The senior engineer shrugged. "Start with a call to his plush Pacific Beach apartment."

But the chief engineer shook his head. "If you want to find Erickson, you go where there's flashy women, fast horses, and high-stakes wagering." He walked back to use the phone in his office. "This may take a while."

Frantic calls were made that ranged the western half of the United States including Del Mar, Santa Anita, Reno, and Las Vegas. After an hour, the chief emerged. "I finally located that high roller over at Century Park. He'd stopped by to return some classified material he'd taken out. He's on his way over."

"Great!" the senior engineer said. He turned and nudged the technician. "In the meantime, take this baby through every emergency activating procedure in the book."

A feverish half hour followed. Finally, after the second repeat of the complicated procedure, an interior phone lit up. The chief, his shirtsleeves rolled up and his necktie undone, quickly grabbed the instrument. "Yeah? It's Erickson, huh? All right, send him up here. What? I don't give a damn if he's got a beautiful dame with him or not! Badge the broad and let her in with him."

The senior wiped at the sweat on his brow. "Thank God Erickson made it!"

"I'll sure as hell roger that!" There was no denying the relief in his voice. "He'll put things right."

Ten minutes later the door to the room opened and a slim, athletic man stepped in. He was obviously the type of individual who spent a lot of time shooting baskets on the court. A leggy, large-breasted, beautiful woman hung on to his arm.

The chief nodded to him. "Hi ya, Erickson. We've been waiting for you."

"What's the trouble then?"

"SCARS is down and won't respond to booting," the senior engineer said. "You designed this baby, so we figure you're the one to put things right."

Erickson turned and winked at the woman. "This won't take long." He pushed the technician aside and took the man's chair. He began a series of input coding, using programming that he had developed with his awesome engineering-design talents. After twenty minutes he knew what was wrong.

"There's interference that's knocked SCARS out," Erickson said. Then he added ominously, "Man-made interference."

The engineers' mouths stood open. It was the chief who recovered first. "But who?"

Erickson stood up. "According to my calculations, the jamming is coming from Southeast Asia." He walked to the woman and turned. "North Vietnam, to be exact."

His female companion cooed at him. "Oh, Genie-kins! You're the greatest!"

"Wait a minute, Erickson!" the chief engineer shouted. "You can't leave us like this!"

Erickson shrugged. "Sorry. There's nothing I can

14

do from here. In fact, there's nothing anyone can do from any distance. That sort of purposeful reception counteraction has to be dealt with at the source."

"You mean someone has to go to North Vietnam to end the problem?"

"Exactly," Erickson said. He turned to the woman and winked. "C'mon, baby. Have I ever taken you to the Denny's by the racetrack?"

"Oooh, Genie-kins!" she exclaimed. "Could we go in your new car this time?"

"You bet," Erickson said. He waved at the men in the communications complex. "Like I said, gentlemen. The only way to solve the problem is to make a personal call right in the middle of an enemy country."

The chief engineer watched Erickson leave, then glanced over at the senior engineer. "Where are they going to find any bastards crazy enough to take on a dangerous job like that?"

Chapter One

Lt. Col. Robert Falconi's Black Eagle Detachment was not able to settle back into a humdrum routine following their harrowing mission that had taken them to the mountains of northern Laos.

Too many unsettling circumstances had descended on them since their return to the base camp at Nui Dep. This was supposed to be a time when they should have been able to unwind. Instead of resting up and enjoying a few cold beers with the new refrigerator their CIA contact had gotten for them, they found they had several situations to deal with.

The first apparent situation had been the disappearance of the detachment scout. Sgt. Archie Dobbs had been having an affair with an Army nurse who was stationed back in Long Binh. He had met her during the time he spent hospitalized from serious injuries sustained during the infiltration phase of Operation Cambodian Challenge. Archie's parachute had failed to open properly and the Black Eagle had plummeted thirteen thousand feet to the jungle floor.

It would have killed anyone else, but as the detachment medic said, "Archie Dobbs didn't have the sense to know he was supposed to have croaked." Then he added with a wry grin, "And when he does buy the farm, the dumb sonofabitch won't know enough to fall down until somebody tells him."

At any rate, while recovering from the injuries, Archie was pampered and babied by an attractive 2nd lieutenant of the Army Nurse Corps named Betty Lou Pemberton. The two fell in love during their time together. Archie's devotion to the young lady was so great that he'd remained faithful to her even when tempted by the sexual favors of exotic, nubile, and willing young women of a Meo hill tribe after he'd returned to active duty. This had occurred during Operation Lord of Laos, when the unit was living with the natives up in the Laotian mountains. His reward for this outstanding fidelity had been an undeserved "Dear John" letter he'd received upon his return from the mission. It seemed that his nurse had found another sweetheart and told Archie that she'd fallen for the new guy in a big way. Archie's reaction was impetuous and unwise. He wanted to talk with Betty Lou, and beat hell out of her new boyfriend. At the first chance, he snuck aboard the earliest available chopper flying back to Saigon.

Thus, for the first time in their existence, the Black Eagles carried a man marked AWOL on their Morning Report.

The consternation caused by Archie's emotional upset was soothed somewhat by the return of the detachment sergeant. Sgt. Major Top Gordon had been seriously wounded during the operation on the

18

Song Cai River. The intrepid senior NCO had been sorely missed, but his complete recovery and return to full duty in the Black Eagles was considered a real boon by everybody.

Another surprise—actually a real shocker—that hit Falconi's men was what had happened to their beloved medic, Sfc. Malpractice McCorckel, while he was away on administrative furlough.

Malpractice had gotten married!

He'd met his bride during Operation Song Cai Duel when she worked as his assistant in the dispensary he'd set up in the river village of Tam Nuroc. Malpractice called her "Jean"—which was his corruption of her real name, Xinh. Despite this misappellation, the two had gotten quite chummy while cutting a slug out of Sgt. Major Top Gordon's chest. This professional experience grew into a more intimate one after Falconi had given both Malpractice and Calvin Culpepper administrative leaves to cool down after ten missions. Calvin had headed for the delights offered in Hong Kong, and Malpractice had hopped a river boat to return to his lady love. The courtship that followed his appearance in Tam Nuroc was brief but effective, and the beautiful young Vietnamese woman became his bride.

The other shocking event, which even caught Lt. Col. Falconi flat-footed, was the unexpected battlefield commission awarded to Master Sgt. Ray Swift Elk. This full-blooded Sioux Indian, who served as the detachment's intelligence sergeant and analyst, had spent a lot of his free time working the Series-Ten Correspondence Course offered by the Infantry School at Fort Benning, Georgia. This "Learn-by-

Mail" instruction was designed to prepare the enlisted man who took it for a reserve infantry commission. Swift Elk, a quiet man with a sharp and deep intellect, had easily mastered the course and passed the final examinations with a record-setting 97% overall grade.

The Army's paperwork mill had slowly ground through its paces and the new qualifications for commission had finally drifted down through channels until it was inserted into Swift Elk's 201-File. Unfortunately, his assignment to a clandestine, bastard unit like the Black Eagles kept any positive action from being taken on this triumph in military education. But finally the CIA field operative who acted as liaison between SOG—the Special Operations Group—and Falconi's unit noticed the Certificate of Completion.

This CIA man, Chuck Fagan, took the evidence of Swift Elk's qualification for officerhood to the Powers-That-Be in SOG and made a pitch for the Indian's lieutenancy. The adjutant, a harried colonel, had made a quick dismissal of the petition.

"Now, Fagin," he'd said with a weary sigh, "Sergeant Swift Elk is not holding an officer's position in the Black Eagle TO."

"TO?" Fagan exclaimed. "Table of Organization? Hell, Colonel, you know as well as I do that the detachment doesn't have a godamned TO! Falconi just arranges the organization to fit his moods and needs. He could have a dozen captains in the detachment if he wanted to."

The colonel's brow knitted in serious consideration. "Isn't he short an officer now?"

"Like I said," Fagin answered. "There isn't any particular number required. But since Lieutenant Hawkins bought it on the last mission, Falconi is the only officer in the detachment."

The colonel nodded. "Mmmm. You sent the poor bastards up where that crazy Frenchman was running an opium empire, didn't you?"

"*I* didn't send them up there, Colonel! SOG pulled that particular boner," Fagin replied hotly. Then, realizing that he would get nowhere pissing off the officer, he calmed down. "Anyhow, that doesn't matter. The point is that right now Falconi doesn't have any other officers with him."

"That could cause an administrative nightmare somewhere down the line," the colonel admitted. "Particularly if something happened to Falconi. Hell, there's lots of paperwork that requires an officer's signature. Let me see Sergeant Swift Elk's records."

Fagin, now knowing the battle was almost won, smiled and handed over the 201-File. "Here you go."

The colonel didn't need to take a lot of time to check out Swift Elk's qualifications. The numerous citations, letters of commendation, and other honors — as well as the extensive Army schooling — spoke for themselves. Once more the colonel sighed. "So I don't have enough to do on top of this?"

"You'll do what's right, Colonel," Fagin said diplomatically. "And I know you won't let a good sergeant down."

"In this case," the colonel remarked, "it would be better to say I won't let a fellow officer down. Don't worry, Fagin. I'll personally see that this is processed through the system."

Thus, Master Sgt. Ray Swift Elk became 2nd Lt. Ray Swift Elk.

When the news arrived at the Black Eagle bunker in Camp Nui Dep, the guys went crazy. There was a rush to salute the new officer to collect the traditional dollar that must be paid when a lieutenant receives this military greeting for the first time. Blue Richards thought he had the honor, but Top Gordon hotly contested the Navy man's claim to the money since he'd impetuously performed the salute indoors.

Calvin Culpepper, an old soldier with plenty of experience, saw his chance. Although they were still inside the bunker, he rushed across the room and pulled up in front of Swift Elk. Snapping to attention, Calvin rendered a salute that would have done credit to a member of the British Brigade of Guards. "Sir!" he bellowed at the top of his baritone voice. "Sergeant Culpepper reporting to the lieutenant!"

Even Sgt. Major Gordon had to admit that it was proper to salute when reporting to an officer—whether it be indoors or outside.

Swift Elk grinned and pulled out his wallet. He produced a greenback and handed it over. "Asshole!"

"You're an asshole too," Calvin said taking the money. Then he quickly added, "Sir!"

That event had taken place in the late afternoon. This gave the detachment plenty of time to celebrate both Malpractice's marriage and Swift Elk's commission. They went all out, even inviting Maj. Rory Riley, the official commandant of Camp Nui Dep, and some of his staff to attend. This was a bit of a sacrifice on the Black Eagles' part. They and Riley's men had been involved in several monumental brawls

22

that had left the participants bruised and bleeding. The majority of these altercations had involved cold beer—or the lack thereof—but there actually was no real lasting animosity between the groups. A case of sincere mutual respect existed there at Camp Nui Dep, and in times of real need and trouble. Lt. Col. Robert Falconi's Black Eagles and Maj. Rory Riley's Green Berets would back each other up to hell and back if necessary.

Once the beer was chilled and the refreshments put out—the buffet was a simple one of GI potato sticks from 5-in-1 rations and crackers and jelly from C-rations—the ceremonial part of the celebration began. The first part of this consisted of a serious toast to Sfc. Malpractice McCorckel wishing him a long and happy marriage.

Then they turned their attention to the new officer.

This portion of the festivities began with Ray Swift Elk going to the head of the room flanked by Falconi and Riley. The ex-master sergeant, grinning shyly, took it all good naturedly.

"Guys," Falconi said addressing the small crowd. "It is my sad duty to demote a damned good non-commissioned officer. Sergeant Swift Elk has served the Black Eagle Detachment in several capacities, and he has always performed his duties in a superlative manner. Mostly he has been our intelligence man, keeping us up to date on enemy activity and what to expect from the bad guys during our operations."

There was some yelling and applause.

"He's also acted as a scout, bravely leading us through dark jungles after the NVA, the Viet Cong, and other villainous bastards," Falconi continued.

Calvin Culpepper guffawed and called out, "Yeah! And he's helped us run from them sumbitches too!"

Falconi joined in the laughter that followed. "He's also been our detachment sergeant when called on for that high assignment too."

Riley, standing with the colonel, feigned puzzlement. "After all that, you're demoting him, sir?"

"I sure am," Falconi replied.

"My God!" Riley cried. "Not down to buck sergeant!"

"Worse than that," Falconi said.

"You mean—" Riley hesitated as he put on an act of being horrified. "Corporal?"

Falcon shook his head and repeated himself. "Worse than that!"

"Oh, shit!" Riley shouted. "You're not going to reduce Sergeant Swift Elk to private, are you?"

"Even worse," Falconi said. "I'm reducing him to—" He paused for dramatic effect, then shouted out, "*Second Lieutenant!*"

Cries of mock horror and rage came from the crowd.

Swift Elk rolled his eyes upward in consternation. "Oh, Jesus! It ain't worth it."

Falconi pulled his Buck knife from the scabbard on his boot. "This is gonna hurt you worse than me," he said with a cackle. He slowly and methodically cut away the master sergeant chevrons from Swift Elk's right sleeve. After they were removed he showed the insignia to the crowd, then tossed it into their midst.

The Black Eagles and Green Berets yelled and pushed each other in wild attempts to stomp on the insignia of rank.

"I oughta make you bastards eat them stripes!" Swift Elk yelled at them as the other set of chevrons was removed and given the same treatment.

Falconi produced a borrowed pair of second lieutenant's gold bars from his pocket. He pinned them to the Sioux Indian's fatigue jacket shoulders, purposely jabbing him.

"Ow!" Swift Elk said instinctively.

"Oh, excuse me!" Falconi said. "I forgot how sensitive officers were." Then he stepped back and made a grand bow to the crowd. "Gentlemen, I introduce to you Second Lieutenant Raymond Swift Elk."

Loud yelling and applause broke out again, this time with cries of "Speech! Speech"

Swift Elk signaled for quiet. "Okay, you guys are having a lot of fun with me," he said. "But this commission is the result of a hell of a lot of work. And even after that, I still had a pretty steep obstacle to get over before they'd make me an officer. In fact, there was a waiver involved, and it's the kind that's almost impossible to get."

Falconi was puzzled. "What waiver was that?"

Swift Elk grinned. "The ones that allowed me to be an officer even though my parents were married!"

Falconi and Riley broke up as the enlisted men expressed both their amusement and agreement with wild yells and applause.

The next step was the "wetting down" of the new lieutenant bars. This was literally what took place. Falconi and Riley each took a can of beer and poured the entire contents over the bars. This was accomplished with some sincere applause and Swift Elk, despite all the kidding, knew he was being given real heartfelt congratulations for his commission.

There was a general rush for the cold beer in the refrigerator. But even this noise was broken up by a shout from the entrance to the bunker.

"Hey!"

All the men turned their heads toward the sound.

Chuck Fagin, the CIA operative, stood in the door holding his canvas briefcase. "Hi ya," he said announcing himself. "I just got in off a chopper from Peterson Field." He looked around the room with a puzzled expression on his face. "What's going on here?"

Falconi looked over the crowd. "We're having a party for Lieutenant Swift Elk."

Fagin checked his watch. "Okay. I'll give you another ten minutes." He raised the briefcase. "I've got an OPLAN here."

"For immediate execution?" Falconi asked.

Fagin smiled without amusement. "Falconi, all my OPLANs are for *immediate* execution."

Chapter Two

The acronym OPLAN, used by Chuck Fagin to refer to the papers in his briefcase, stood for Operations Plan.

An OPLAN is a brief concept of how a scheduled operation or mission should be conducted. The particular one that Fagin carried into the bunker in Camp Nui Dep had been aptly designated as *OPLAN Operation Dien Bien Phu Encore.* An OPLAN was written by the staff at Special Operations Group in Saigon when they wanted a specific job carried out. Even at that high level, it was not considered to be "etched in stone." Instead, it was a set of guidelines and information supplied to Lt. Col. Robert Falconi and his men so that they could assimiliate the information supplied and add their own input along with other data to create another, much more authoritative paper that would be called the OPORD (Operation Order).

The OPORD was written along strict guidelines that divided it into five basic paragraphs, as follows:

1. SITUATION

   a. Enemy Forces: (This was the strength, activity, identification, etc., of the bad guys that Falconi and his men were going to face.)

   b. Friendly Forces: (These were the good joes that would be participating—or at least be located damned close—to them during the operation. This included special notes on support capabilities, coordination, cooperation, etc. In most Black Eagle missions this paragraph was labeled N/A—Not Applicable—since the detachment would be out in the boonies operating on its own.)

2. MISSION

   (A simple statement saying exactly what the Black Eagles were supposed to accomplish.)

3. EXECUTION

   a. Concept of the Operation: (The "How-It's-Gonna-Be-Done" paragraph, which included times, dates, organization, specific duties, etc.)

4. ADMINISTRATION AND LOGISTICS

   a. Rations

   b. Arms and Ammunition

   c. Uniforms and Equipment

   d. Special (Handling of wounded, prisoners, etc.)

5. COMMAND AND SIGNAL

   a. Signal: (Equipment, call signs, etc.)

   b. Command: (The chain of command.)

Now, crowded into Falconi's small office in the bunker, the lieutenant colonel, Ray Swift Elk, and Fagin each held a copy of the OPLAN. Out in the squad bay, the rest of the detachment had their own OPLANs and were carefully reading them. This small document was the nucleus of a planning activity that had begun when Swift Elk's promotion party had been brought to a swift and undignified end.

OPLAN Dien Bien Phu Encore was the official announcement that an operation was about to go down. It would be up to the Black Eagles to make all final decisions on how they would conduct the assigned mission. These finer points would be added to the OPLAN in annexes written by the men. These would include the Supply Annex, Intelligence Annex, Infiltration Annex, Exfiltration Annex, etc. Specific individuals, according to their specialties, would be assigned to write these annexes and submit them to Lt. Col. Falconi for his approval. For example, Staff Sgt. Paulo Garcia, as the detachment intelligence sergeant, would write the Intelligence Annex; the supply sergeant, Hank Valverde, would do the Supply Annex; Malpractice McCorckel had the Medical Annex—with others performing the remaining necessary chores in the endeavor. It is not surprising therefore that, besides all the tough-guy qualifications needed to become a Black Eagle, there was also a requirement to be able to type.

But before this activity began, Falconi and Swift Elk had to milk Fagin's brain to fill in any empty holes in this preliminary plan.

"Okay, Fagin," Falconi said setting his OPLAN aside. "Give us the poop in your own words and we'll take it from there."

"Right," Fagin said. "The bottom line is this: the Russkies have set up a satellite-communications jamming station in North Vietnam to screw up our programs in space."

Swift Elk, still soaking in beer from having his bars wetted down, doodled on his own OPLAN as he spoke. "What exact point in North Vietnam is this place located?"

"Near Dien Bien Phu. But we can't pinpoint the *exact* place," Fagin said. "I know it's a hell of a hairy location to hit and get out of, but that's what the Reds are banking on. We also figure it's made them complacent enough not to expect any trouble."

Falconi lit a cigarette and leaned back in his chair. "I can understand their self-assurance, Fagin. We can get into the place with no sweat. But once on the ground there's no goddamned way we can possibly find our way around. Even the latest maps available from SOG S2 won't be up to date enough to help us out."

"That fucking Archie!" Swift Elk swore. "He's the only guy in the unit who could smell out the place. Of all the times to go AWOL!"

"Yeah," Falconi agreed angrily. "He's really let us down with that shitty attitude of his."

"No sweat. We have an asset for you," Fagin said.

Swift Elk was not impressed. "We won't get much help out of some local yokel that's been recruited with a million or so piasters, Fagin. A sonofabitch like that couldn't be trusted enough to risk the lives of sixteen good men."

Fagin wagged a finger. "You're too suspicious, Ray. This particular asset is completely trustworthy and has been inserted into the area only a couple of weeks ago. She was born and raised in that part of the country and knows every gulley and hill around the place."

Falconi snapped a surprised glance at Fagin. *"She!"*

Fagin hesitated. "Yeah, Falconi. And you know her." He nervously rubbed his hand across his chin. "It's Andrea Thuy."

"Andrea!" Falconi exclaimed.

Swift Elk sucked in his breath. "Jesus!"

"Goddamn you, Fagin! You told me she was back in the States, completely out of the game," Falconi said angrily. "You even said she was going to college and building a new life."

Fagin took a deep breath. "I was given that same information, Falconi. But I didn't believe it for an instant. And I don't think you really did either. There's no way the Agency would let a good operative like that get away."

Falconi's emotions went into a tailspin. Andrea Thuy, the beautiful Eurasian daughter of a French doctor and a Vietnamese mother, had been the only woman he'd ever loved. Losing her when she'd left Southeast Asia had been one of the most painful moments of his life. But his heartache had been smoothed a great deal with the knowledge that she was at least finally out of danger and living a safe existence in the United States. This sudden realization that she was not only still a CIA agent, but was awaiting the arrival of the Black Eagle detachment in North Vietnam, caught him mentally unprepared.

"I'm sorry to spring this on you, Falconi," Fagin said sincerely. "But there was no way I could ease it out."

31

"Okay! Okay!" Falconi said irritably as he regained control of his feelings. "We have a job to do. Let's get on with it."

"If it's any comfort to you, this operation is going to be one of the best-planned, best-monitored missions you guys have ever been on," Fagin said.

Swift Elk snorted. "You mean it won't be one of our regular run-of-the-mill cluster fucks that you always get us into."

"Don't exaggerate," Fagin said.

"Exaggerate!" Falconi yelled. "You sonofabitch! It wasn't too long ago your planning ended up with our backs pinned down in front of a cliff in Cambodia out of ammo and water."

"Yeah," Fagin countered, "But you weren't out of luck."

Swift Elk frowned. "If it hadn't been for Archie Dobbs coming in with that chopper we'd be pushing up daisies right now instead of sitting here with you."

"Hey, guys!" Fagin protested. "It's all part of the plan."

"What about on the Song Cai?" Falconi asked. "You got us out on the goddamned river outnumbered and outgunned."

"And who showed up with quad-fifties to turn the tide?" Fagin asked. "Me—*me!* That's who."

"If you'd made that dramatic fucking appearance fifteen minutes later we'd have been at the bottom of the muddy body of water," Falconi reminded him. "You're the classic example of P.P.P.P.P.P.P. — Piss-Poor Prior Planning Prevents Positive Projects," Falconi said.

"It's always worked out in the end," Fagin said.

"I've got some figures in my head," Falconi said. "So far there's been a total of fifty-two guys who've served in this detachment. Of that number, thirty-six have been killed. That's a casualty rate of almost seventy percent."

"In my book that ain't good," Swift Elk interjected. "So let's not talk about things always turning out all right in the end."

Fagin sighed. "I'm sorry. What more can I say? I'm sorry."

"Yeah. Now I've got Andrea to worry about again," Falconi said.

Swift Eagle, realizing that Falconi needed some time alone, stood up. "We've been jawing enough. I'll go give the guys a preliminary briefing and arrange for Isolation with Rory Riley."

"Thanks, Ray," Falconi said.

"I'll go with you," Fagin said artfully. The two went out to set things up and get the Isolation Phase into full swing.

The term "Isolation" could be taken literally. During this time the Black Eagles, following Special Forces procedures, were isolated away from the rest of Camp Nui Dep. Barbed wire would be strung around the area and Maj. Rory Riley provided guards to make sure nobody got in or out without proper authority. This was security in the strictest sense. No one was trusted. Not even the Green Berets who shared Nui Dep with the Black Eagles.

During this time, however, the only individuals who would come and go with any frequency would be Lt. Col. Falconi and the supply sergeant, Valverde. Both had double-duty in administrative red

33

tape.

Within one hour the detachment was in full Isolation. Several briefings and discussions of the OPLAN were held. Once all this available information was brought together it was hashed, rehashed, and re-rehashed. Only then, and when it was set down on paper, would it receive the final blessing from the Reverend Lt. Col. Robert Falconi. That was the moment it could finally be considered etched in the proverbial stone.

The men drew off in their groups according to teams and jobs. It was important that each sub-unit understand its particular role in the various phases of the mission, and there were individual responsibilities too.

Falconi had the biggest headache. He was the one charged with the actual working out of the execution phase. He had to figure times, distances, and methods for destroying the jamming station. As he'd told Fagin, getting into the place was easy. All they had to do was fly over North Vietnam and parachute in. That was no big deal. The map gave indications of several good isolated areas to use as drop zones. The other two problems were the brain-teasers.

Falconi had to decide whether to simply shoot their way into the place and blow the hell out of it, or perhaps sneak a couple of guys in to plant explosives and detonate the boom-boom stuff with timing devices. Either way called for several conferences with his chief advisors—2d Lt. Ray Swift Elk and Sgt. Major Top Gordon. He also had to get some technical data from his demolitions experts Calvin Culpepper and Blue Richards.

34

Then Lt. Col. Robert Falconi had to perform the loneliest and most frightening job of a commander—make decisions that would either make or break the mission. This was more than Succeed-or-Fail, it was Do-or-Die.

Falconi bent over the latest maps and the only layout he had of the target. This latter was a sketch map sent out of the operational area by Andrea Thuy. She had quickly drawn it, then used a series of deadletter drops to send it south. The sight of her small, careful handwriting caused painful memories for Falconi as he recalled love letters they'd exchanged during their passionate affair.

At the same time the others kept at their work. Fresh ideas, or changes in previous ones from their commander, caused alterations in their own work. Calvin and Blue recalculated various charges and detonators as Falconi's fertile brain worked out the way he wanted to get the job done.

Typewriters clacked, ammunition was issued, men cursed, coffee was consumed, and numerous little meetings occurred as the men worked harder and faster to get ready to go on their dangerous journey.

Hank Valverde, the supply man, spent an entire night filling out requisitions for special equipment. As he was about to submit them through Maj. Rory Riley's staff, Falconi called him in and gave him a whole new concept of the operation. Hank displayed a weak smile, tore up all his paperwork, and started from scratch.

But in thirty hours' time the preparation phase was completed. The guys, with their equipment ready, sat apprehensively in the squad bay waiting for Falconi

35

to emerge from his office.

The lieutenant colonel stepped out. "We'll take a ten-minute break outside for some fresh air," he announced. "Then we'll start the briefing."

There was one large, collective sigh, and the men filed up the steps of the bunker for a brief rest in the hot, humid air outside.

Chapter Three

The Black Eagles did not suddenly spring into being. They were the brainchild of a Central Intelligence Agency case officer named Clayton Andrews. And that man snarled and kicked through knotted red tape for months before he finally received the official okay to turn his concept of creating an independent band of jungle fighters into a living, breathing, ass-kicking reality.

In those early days of the 1960s, "Think Tanks" of Ph.D.s at various centers of American political thought and study were conducting mental wrestling matches with the question of fighting Communism in southeast Asia. Andrews was involved in that same program, but in a tremendously more physical way — Andrews was in combat. And he participated in more than just a small amount of clandestine fighting in that part of the world. He hit it in a big way, which included a hell of a lot of missions that went beyond mere harassment operations in Viet Cong areas. His main job was the conduct of penetrations into North Vietnam itself. When this dangerous assignment, because of numerous blunders, cost plenty of good men their lives, Andrews began his battle with the stodgy military administration to set things up properly. It took diplomatic persuasion—combined with a few ferocious outbreaks of temper—before the program was eventually expanded. When that happened, Andrews was suddenly thrust into a position where he needed not simply an *excellent* combat commander—he needed the *best*. Thus, he began an extensive search for an officer to lead that special detachment which would carry out certain down-and-dirty missions. After hundreds of investigations and interviews, he settled on a Special Forces captain named Robert Falconi.

Pulling all the strings he had, Andrews saw to it that the Green Beret officer was transferred to his own branch of SOG—the Special Operations Group—to begin work on this brand-new project.

Capt. Falconi was tasked with organizing a new fighting unit to be known as the Black Eagles. This group's basic policy was to be primitive and simple: seek out the enemy and kill the sons of bitches.

Their mission was to penetrate deep into the heartland of the Communists to disrupt, destroy, maim, and slay. The men who would belong to the Black Eagles would be volunteers from every branch of the armed forces. And that was to include all nationalities involved in the struggle against the Red invasion of South Vietnam.

Each man was to be an absolute master in his particular brand of military mayhem. He had to be an expert in not only his own nation's firearms but also those of other friendly and enemy countries. But the required knowledge in weaponry didn't stop at the modern types. It also included knives, bludgeons, garrotes, and even crossbows for when the need to deal silent death arose.

There was also a requirement for the more sophisticated and peaceful skills too. Foreign languages, land navigation, communications, medicine, and even mountaineering and scuba diving were to be within the realm of knowledge of the Black Eagles. Then, in addition, each man had to know how to type. In an outfit that had no clerks, this office skill was extremely important because each had to do his own paperwork. Much of this involved operations orders that directed their highly complicated, dangerous missions. These documents had to be legible and easy to read in order to avoid confusing, deadly errors in combat.

The Black Eagles became the enforcement arm of SOG, drawing the missions which were the most dangerous and sensitive. In essence they were hit men, closely coordinated and completely dedicated, held together and directed through the forceful personality of their leader, Capt. Robert Falconi.

After Clayton Andrews was promoted out of the job, a new CIA officer moved in. This was Chuck Fagin. An ex-paratrooper and veteran of both World War II and the Korean War, Fagin had a natural talent when it came to dreaming up nasty things to do to the unfriendlies up north. It didn't take him long to get Falconi and his boys busy.

Their first efforts were directed against a pleasure palace in North Vietnam. This bordello *par excellence* was used by Communist officials during their retreats from the trials and tribulations of administering authority and regulations over their slave populations. There were no excesses, perverted tastes, or

39

unusual demands that went unsatisfied in this hidden fleshpot.

Falconi and his wrecking crew skydived into the operations area in a HALO (High Altitude Low Opening) infiltration, and when the Black Eagles finished their raid on the whorehouse, there was hardly a soul left alive to continue the debauchery.

Their next hell-trek into the enemy's hinterlands was an even more dangerous assignment with the difficulty factor multiplied by the special demands placed on them. The North Vietnamese had set up a special prison camp in which they were perfecting their skills in the torture-interrogation of downed American pilots. With the conflict escalating in Southeast Asia, they rightly predicted they would soon have more than just a few Yanks in their hands. A North Korean brainwashing expert had come down from his native country to teach them the fine points of mental torment. He had learned his despicable trade during the Korean War when he had had American POWs directly under his control. His use of psychological torture, combined with just the right amount of physical torment, had broken more than one man despite the most spirited resistance. Experts who studied his methods came to the conclusion that only a completely insane prisoner, whose craziness caused him to ignore both the sensation of pain and the instinct for survival, could have resisted the North Korean's methods.

At the time of the Black Eagles' infiltration into North Vietnam, the prisoners behind the barbed wire were few—but important. A U.S.A.F. pilot, an Army Special Forces sergeant, and two high-ranking officers of the South Vietnamese forces were the unwilling tenants of the concentration camp.

Falconi and his men were not only tasked to rescue the POWs, they also had to bring along the prison's commandant and his North Korean tutor. Falconi pulled off the job, fighting his way south through the North Vietnamese Army and Air Force to a bloody showdown on the Song Bo River. The situation deteriorated to the point where the Black Eagles' magazines were down to their last few rounds as they waited for the NVA's final charge. But the unexpected and spirited aid from anti-Communist guerrillas turned the tide, and the Black Eagles smashed their way out of the encirclement.

The next operation took them to Laos, where they were pitted against the fanatical savages of the Pathet Lao. If that wasn't bad enough, their method of entrance into the operational area was bizarre and dangerous. The type of transport into battle hadn't been used in active combat in more than twenty years. It had even been labeled obsolete by military experts. But this didn't deter the Black Eagles.

They used a glider to make a silent flight to a secret landing zone. If that weren't bad enough, the operations plan called for their extraction through a glider-recovery apparatus that not only hadn't been tested in combat, but had never even been given sufficient trial under rehearsed, safe conditions.

After a hairy ride in the flimsy craft, they hit the ground to carry out a mission designed to destroy the construction site of a Soviet nuclear power plant the Reds wanted to install in the area. Everything went wrong from the start, and the Black Eagles fought against a horde of insane zealots until their extraction to safety. This was completely dependent on the illegal and unauthorized efforts of a dedicated U.S.A.F. pilot — the same one they had rescued from the North Vietnam prison camp. The Air Force colonel was determined to help the same men who had saved him, and he came through with all pistons firing, paying the debt he owed Falconi's guys.

This hairy episode was followed by two occurrences. The first was Capt. Robert Falconi's promotion to major, and the second was a mission that was doubly dangerous because of the impossibility of making firm operation plans. Unknown Caucasian personnel, posing as U.S. troops, had been committing atrocities against Vietnamese peasants. The situation had gotten far enough out of control that the effectiveness of American efforts in the area had been badly damaged. Once again Falconi and the Black Eagles were called in to put things right. They went in on a dark beach from a submarine and began a determined reconnaissance until they finally made contact with their quarry.

These enemy agents, wearing U.S. Army uniforms, were dedicated East German Communists prepared to fight to the death for their cause. The Black Eagles admired such unselfish dedication so much that they gave the Reds the opportunity to accomplish their end: sacrifice their lives for Communism.

But not without the situation deteriorating to the point where the Black Eagles had to endure human-wave assaults from a North Vietnamese army battalion led by an infuriated general. This officer had been humiliated by Falconi on the Song Bo River several months previously. The mission ended in another Black Eagle victory, but not before five more good men had died.

Brought back to Saigon at last, the seven survivors of the previous operations cleaned their weapons, drew fresh, clean uniforms, and prepared for a long-awaited period of R&R—Rest and Recreation.

It was not to be.

Chuck Fagin's instincts and organizations of agents had ferreted out information that showed a high-ranking intelligence officer of the South Vietnamese Army had been leaking information on the Black Eagles to his superiors up in the Communist North. It would have been easy enough to arrest this double agent, but an entire enemy espionage net had been involved. Thus, Falconi and his Black Eagles had to come in from the boondocks and fight the good fight against these spies and assassins in the back streets of Saigon itself.

When Saigon was relatively cleaned up, the Black Eagles drew a mission that involved going out on the Ho Chi Minh Trail on which the North Vietnamese sent supplies, weapons, and munitions south to be used by the Viet Cong and elements of the North Vietnamese Army. The enemy was enjoying great success despite repeated aerial attacks by the U.S. and South Vietnamese air forces. The high command decided that only a sustained campaign conducted on the ground would put a crimp in the Reds' operation.

Naturally, they chose the Black Eagles for the dirty job.

Falconi and his men waged partisan warfare in its most primitive and violent fashion with raids, am-

43

bushes, and other forms of jungle fighting. The order of the day was "kill or be killed" as the monsoon forest thundered with reports of numerous types of modern weaponry. This dangerous situation was made even more deadly by a decidedly insidious and deadly form of mine warfare which made each track and trail through the brush a potential zone of death.

When this was wrapped up, Falconi and his troops received an even bigger assignment. This next operation involved working with Chinese mercenaries to secure an entire province ablaze with infiltration and invasion by the North Vietnamese Army. This also involved beautiful Andrea Thuy, a lieutenant in the South Vietnamese Army who had been attached to the Black Eagles. Playing on the mercenaries' superstitions and religion, she became a "warrior-sister" leading some of the blazing combat herself.

An affair of honor followed this mission, when Red agents kidnapped this lovely woman. They took her north—but not for long. Falconi and the others pulled a parachute-borne attack and brought her out of the hellhole where her Communist tormentors had put her.

The ninth mission, pulled off with most of the detachment's veterans away on R&R, involved a full-blown attack by North Vietnamese regulars into the II Corps area—all this while the Black Eagles were saddled with a pushy newspaper reporter.

By that time South Vietnam had rallied quite a number of allies to her side. Besides the United States, there was South Korea, Australia, New Zealand, the Philippines, and Thailand. This situation upset the Communist side, and they decided to counter it by openly having various Red countries send contingents of troops to bolster the NVA (North Vietnamese Army) and the Viet Cong.

This resulted in a highly secret situation — ironically well-known by both the American and Communist sides — which developed in the borderland between Cambodia and South Vietnam. The Reds, in an effort to make their war against the Americans a truly international struggle, began an experimental operation involving volunteers from Algeria. These young Arab Communists, led by hardcore Red officers, were to be tested against U.S. troops. If they proved effective, other nationalities would be brought in from behind the Iron Curtain to expand the insurgency against the Americans, South Vietnamese, and their allies.

Because of the possibility of failure, the Reds did not want to publicize these "volunteers" to the conflict unless the experiment proved a rousing success. The American brass also did not want the situation publicized under any circumstances. To do so would be to play into the world-opinion manipulations of the Communists.

But the generals in Saigon wanted the situation neutralized as quickly as possible.

Thus, Falconi and the Black Eagles moved into the jungle to take on the Algerians led by the fanatical Major Omar Ahmed. Ahmed, who had rebelled against France in Algeria, had actually fought in the French Army in Indochina as an enemy of the very people he'd ended up serving. Captured before the Battle of Dien Bien Phu, he had been an easy and pliable subject for the Red brainwashers and interrogators. When he returned to his native Algeria after repatriation, he was a dedicated Communist ready to take on anything the Free World could throw at him.

Falconi and his men, with their communications system destroyed by deceit, fought hard. But they were badly outnumbered and finally forced into the situation where their backs were literally pinned against the wall of a jungle cliff. Until Archie Dobbs, injured on the infiltration jump and evacuated from the mission back to the U.S. Army hospital at Long Binh, went AWOL in order to rejoin his buddies in combat. He successfully returned to them, arriving in a helicopter gunship that threw in the fire support necessary to turn the situation around.

The Communist experiment was swept away in the volleys of aerial fire and the final bayonet charge of the Black Eagles. The end result was a promotion to lieutenant colonel for Robert Falconi, while his senior non-coms also were given a boost up the Army's career ladder. But Archie Dobbs, who had gone AWOL from the hospital, was demoted.

After Operation Cambodian Challenge, the Black Eagles only received the briefest of rests back at their base garrison. They returned to Camp Nui Dep with fond hopes of R&R dancing through their combat-buzzed minds, only to be interrupted by the next challenge to their courage and ingenuity. This was a mission that was dubbed Operation Song Cai Duel.

Communist patrol boats had infiltrated the Song Cai River and controlled that waterway north of Dak Bla. Their activities ranged from actual raiding of river villages and military outposts, to active operations involving the transportation and infiltration of Red agents.

This Red campaign resulted in putting the Song Cai River, in South Vietnam, under the complete control of Ho Chi Minh's fighters. They virtually owned the waterway.

The brass's orders to Falconi were simple. *Get the river back!*

The mission, however, was much more complicated. Distances were long, logistics difficult, and personnel in short supply. But that had never stopped the Black Eagles before.

There were new lessons to be learned too. River navigation, powerboating, and amphibious warfare had to be added to the Black Eagles' skills in jungle fighting.

Outgunned and outnumbered, Falconi and his guys waded in over their heads. The pressure mounted to the point where the village they used as a base headquarters had to be evacuated. But a surprise appearance by Chuck Fagin with a couple of quad-fifty machine guns turned the tide.

The final showdown was a gunboat battle that turned the muddy waters of the Song Cai red with blood.

It was pure hell for the men, but it was another brick laid in the wall of their brief and glorious history.

The next Black Eagle adventure began on a strange note. A French intelligence officer, who was a veteran of France's Indochinese War, was attached to SOG in an advisory role. While visiting the communications room, he was invited to listen in on an intermittent radio transmission in the French language that the section had been monitoring for several months. When he heard it, the Frenchman was astounded. The broadcast was from a French soldier who correctly identified himself through code as a member of the G.M.I. (*Groupement Mixte d'Intervention*), which had been carrying on guerrilla warfare utilizing native volunteers in the old days.

Contact was made, and it was learned that this Frenchman was indeed a G.M.I. veteran who had been reported missing in action during mountain insurgency operations in 1953. And he'd done more than just survive for fifteen years. He was the leader of a large group of Meo tribesmen who were actively raiding into North Vietnam from Laos.

The information was kicked "upstairs" and the brass hats became excited. Not only was this man a proven ass-kicker, he could also provide valuable intelligence and an effective base of operations to launch further missions into the homeland of the Reds. It was officially decided to make contact with the man and bring him into the "Big Picture" by supplying him with arms, equipment, and money to continue his war against the communists. The G3 Section also thought it would be a great idea to send in a detachment of troops to work with him.

They chose Lt. Col. Robert Falconi and his Black Eagles for the job.

But when the detachment infiltrated the operational area they did not find a dedicated anti-Communist. Instead, they were faced with an insane French army sergeant named Farouche, who reigned over an opium empire high in the Laotian mountains.

48

He had contacted the allies only for added weaponry and money in his crazy plans to wrest power from other warlords.

The mission dissolved into sheer hell. Falconi and the guys not only had to travel by foot back through five hundred miles of enemy territory to reach the safety of friendly lines, they also had to fight both the Communists and Farouche's tribesmen every step of the way.

The effort cost them three good men, and when they finally returned to safety, Archie Dobbs found that his nurse sweetheart had left him for another man. Enraged and broken-hearted, the detachment scout took off AWOL to track down his lady love and her boyfriend.

Falconi also expanded his Table of Organization and built up another fire team to give the detachment a grand total of three. Ray Swift Elk was commissioned an officer and made second-in-command, Sgt. Major Top Gordon was released from the hospital, and Malpractice McCorckel and Calvin Culpepper returned from furlough. Six new men were added to the roster so that, despite Archie Dobbs's disappearance, the detachment was in damned good shape numerically.

It was to the Black Eagles' credit that unit integrity and morale always seemed to increase after each operation despite the staggering losses they suffered. Not long after their inception, the detachment decided they wanted an insignia all their own. This wasn't at all unusual for units in Vietnam. Local manufacturers, acting on designs submitted to them by the troops involved, produced these emblems, which were worn by the outfits while "in country." These adornments were strictly nonregulation and unauthorized for display outside Vietnam.

Falconi's men came up with a unique beret badge manufactured as a cloth insignia. A larger version was used as a shoulder patch. The design consisted of a black eagle—naturally—with spread wings. The big bird's beak was opened in a defiant battle cry, and he clutched a sword in one claw and a bolt of lightning in the other. Mounted on a khaki shield that was trimmed in black, the device was an accurate portrayal of its wearers: somber and deadly.

There was one more touch of their individuality that they kept to themselves. It was a motto which not only worked as a damned good password in hairy situations, but also described the Black Eagles' basic philosophy.

Those special words, in Latin, were:

CALCITRA CLUNIS!

This phrase, in the language of the ancient Romans, translated as: KICK ASS!

said. He looked at Fagin. "Will our aircraft arrive as planned? I at least have to know for sure when we're leaving here."

"That is as written," Fagin announced.

"Does that firm up the time plan?" Swift Elk asked. "I gotta know to lay on some stuff with Hank Valverde."

"You can move on that now," Falconi answered. He took a quick look at his new second-in-command.

Ray Swift Elk, a full-blooded Sioux Indian, was lean and muscular. His copper-colored skin, hawkish nose, and high cheek bones gave him the appearance of the classic prairie warrior. There were still dark spots on his fatigues where he'd removed his master sergeant chevrons. Brand-new cloth insignia of an infantry lieutenant were sewn on his collars.

Twelve years of service in Special Forces had made Swift Elk particularly well-qualified to be the detachment executive officer. Despite his skills and education in modern soldiering, he still considered his ancestral past an important part of his life, and he practiced Indian customs when and where able. Part of his tribe's history included some vicious combat against the black troopers in the U.S. Cavalry's 9th and 10th Regiments of the racially segregated Army of the 19th century. The Sioux warriors had nicknamed the black men they fought "Buffalo Soldiers." This was because of their hair, which, to the Indians, was like the thick manes on the buffalo. The appellation was a sincere compliment due to these native Americans' veneration of the bison. Ray Swift Elk called both black guys in the detachment—Calvin

Culpepper and Dwayne Simpson—"Buffalo Soldiers," and he did so with the same respect his ancestors had used during the Plains Wars.

Falconi lit a cigarette and swung his eyes to study the rugged, dark features of Sgt. Major Gordon. As the senior non-commissioned officer of the Black Eagles, he was tasked with several pre-operational responsibilities. Besides having to take the OPLAN and use it to form the basic OPORD for the missions, he was also responsible for maintaining discipline and efficiency within the unit. Top had been severely wounded during the fighting on the Song Cai River, and only the timely surgery performed by Sfc Malpractice McCorckel had saved his life. He was now fully recovered and itching to get back into action. Top was a husky man, his jet-black hair thinning perceptively, looking even more sparse because of the strict GI haircut he wore.

Gordon's entrance into the Black Eagles had been less than satisfactory. After seventeen years spent in the Army's elite spit-and-polish airborne infantry units, he had brought in an attitude that did not fit well with the diverse individuals in Falconi's command. Gordon's zeal to follow Army regulations to the letter had cost him a marriage when his wife, fed up with having a husband who thought more of the Army than her, filed for divorce and took their kids back to the old hometown in upstate New York. Despite that heartbreaking experience, he hadn't let up a bit. To make things worse in the Black Eagles, he had taken the place of a popular detachment sergeant who was killed in action on the Song Bo River. This noncom, called "Top" by the men, was an

53

old Special Forces man who knew how to handle the type of soldier who volunteered for unconventional units. The new top sergeant would have been resented no matter what type of man he was.

Gordon's first day in his new assignment brought him into quick conflict with the Black Eagle personnel, and it soon got so far out of hand that Falconi began to seriously consider relieving the sergeant and seeing to his transfer back to a regular airborne unit.

But during Operation Laos Nightmare, Gordon's bravery under fire earned him the grudging respect of the lower-ranking Black Eagles. Finally, when he fully realized the problems he had created for himself, he changed his methods of leadership. Gordon backed off doing things by the book and found he could still maintain good discipline and efficiency while getting rid of the chicken-shit aspects of Army life. It was most apparent he had been accepted by the men when they bestowed the nickname "Top" on him.

He had truly become the "top sergeant" then.

Falconi took a final drag on his cigarette and snuffed it out on the ashtray in front of him. "Okay, Top," he said to the sergeant major. "Let's get this briefing on the road."

"Yes, sir," Top Gordon said. He left the small office and went up the steps of the bunker. Outside he found the men sprawled around the small area behind the barbed wire. They spoke together lethargically in low tones. A couple were napping to get rid of the fatigue built up by the long hours of preparing the OPORD. "Break's over," Top announced. "Let's get inside for the briefing."

Surprisingly, the first men to move down to the bunker was the detachment's slowest, easiest-going guy. Petty Officer Blue Richards was a fully qualified Navy Seal. A red-haired Alabaman with a gawky, good-natured grin common to good ol' country boys, Blue had been named after his "daddy's favorite huntin' dawg." An expert in demolitions either on land or underwater, Blue considered himself honored that his father had given him the dog's name.

The next man was Marine Staff Sgt. Paulo Garcia. Under the new reorganization of the detachment, Paulo performed the intelligence work for the Black Eagles. Of Portuguese descent, this former tuna fisherman from San Diego, California, had joined the Marines at the relatively late age of twenty-one after deciding to look for a bit of adventure. There was always Marine Corp activity to see around his hometown, and he decided that that fighting group offered him exactly what he was looking for. Ten years of service and plenty of combat action in the Demilitarized Zone and Khe Sanh had made him more than qualified for the Black Eagles.

The unit's supply sergeant was a truly talented and enterprising staff sergeant named Enrique "Hank" Valverde. He had been in the Army for ten years. Hank began his career as a supply clerk, quickly finding ways to cut through Army red tape to get logistical chores taken care of quickly and efficiently. He made the rank of sergeant in the very short time of only two years, finally volunteering for the Green Berets in the late 1950s. Hank Valverde found that Special Forces was the type of unit that offered him the finest opportunity to hone and practice his legendary supply expertise.

Sgt. Dwayne Simpson, one of the two men called "Buffalo Soldier" by Swift Elk, certainly had family connections to the nickname. A black man from Arizona, his family had served in both the segregated Army of the 19th and early 20th centuries and the modern integrated service for four generations. He was a qualified Ranger with a solid ten years of service to back up his expertise as a heavy-weapons specialist.

A Navy corpsman, Doc Robichaux was a Cajun born and bred in Louisiana. He, like Blue Richards, had a good background in the Seals. He'd spent plenty of time in the "Brown Water Navy" and had also seen combat with Marine infantry units. A short, swarthy young man, he had a friendly face and could play a fiddle that would make a Louisiana Saturday night jump till dawn. Although assigned as a rifleman, he would be expected to help Malpractice McCorckel in medical activities when needed.

Sfc. Calvin Culpepper was a tall, brawny black man who had entered the Army off a poor Georgia farm his family had worked as sharecroppers. Although now a team leader in the detachment, he formerly handled all the demolition chores. His favorite tool in that line of work was C4 plastic explosive. It was said he could set off a charge under a silver dollar and get back nine-nine cents change. Resourceful, intelligent, and combat-wise, Calvin, the other "Buffalo Soldier," pulled his weight—and then a bit more—in the dangerous undertakings of the Black Eagles.

The detachment medic, Sfc Malcomb "Malpractice" McCorckel, came into the bunker on Calvin's heels. An inch under six feet in height, Malpractice had been in the Army for twelve years. He had a friendly face and spoke softly as he pursued his duties seeing after the illnesses and hurts of his buddies. He nagged and needled to keep that wild bunch healthy. They bitched back at him, but not angrily, because each Black Eagle appreciated his concern. They all knew that nothing devised by puny men could keep Malpractice from reaching a wounded detachment member and pulling him back to safety.

The first of the new men now filed down to the briefing area. Although this was officially designated as Sergeant Gunnar Olson's first Black Eagle mission, he'd served with them before. During the operation on the Song Cai River he'd been a gunner—appropriately called Gunnar the Gunner—on a helicopter gunship that flew fire support operations for Falconi and his men. Gunnar was so impressed with the detachment that he immediately put in for a transfer to the unit. Falconi quickly approved the paperwork and hired Gunnar the Gunner on as the unit's machine gunner. Now, armed with an M60 machine gun, Gunnar, of Norwegian descent from Minnesota, looked forward to his new work assignment.

Tiny Burke, who acted as Gunnar's ammo bearer, was the lowest-ranking member of the unit. He was not really qualified mentally for the Green Berets or Black Eagles, but this big, hulking guy had been Gunnar's loader in their helicopter outfit. Not real bright, he made up for his lack of brainpower with physical strength, devotion, and bull-like bravery. Tiny stood six feet, four inches tall and weighed in at a muscular 235 pounds. The ammo cans he carried looked like tin pill boxes in his huge mitts.

Another new man, Sergeant Jesse Makalue, was from Hawaii. Almost as big as Tiny, he was a great natural athlete who could have gotten himself a cushy job participating in a variety of sports at some of the larger Army posts. But Jesse liked danger and both shooting and hitting people. Referees' whistles always pissed him off due to his dislike of any interference with his violence. He was a steady NCO, but had a vicious temper that demanded a lot of control on his part.

Jesse was trailed by Navy Petty Officer 1st Class Sparks Johnson. As Falconi's communications chief, he served under an ominous tradition. He was the fourth man in the job and, like all the others, was Navy. All his predecessors—Petty Officers Fred Jackson, Durwood Martin, and Leland Brewster—had not survived more than three Black Eagle missions. Falconi had fully appraised Sparks of the jinks on the job, but the Seal had only shrugged. "There ain't nobody supposed to live forever."

Falconi was glad to have him aboard.

The U.S. Marine Corps' latest contribution to the Black Eagles was Staff Sgt. Salty O'Rourke. This ageless wonder had over twenty-five years of service. Salty kept himself in outstanding physical condition and had been known as one of the toughest drill instructors in the corps. By rights, Salty should have been a sergeant major—or at least a gunnery sergeant—but his rather marked lack of social finesse and tendency to settle things with his fists kept him from moving into the more elite non-commissioned-officer positions in the headquarters of higher-echelon units.

The final man down in the bunker was Sgt. Dean Fotopoulus. A Greek-American from Chicago, he'd moved from the sport of wrestling, where he'd had a college scholarship, to the martial art of karate. His devotion to this skill had earned him a black belt, and the discipline learned from it made Special Forces seem attractive. Now, with seven years of service, he was looking forward to this newest phase of his military career.

Falconi stood by the door as the men came in one by one and took the chairs arranged there. The colonel loved those guys despite the outward coolness he displayed toward them. His soldier's heart had broken with each of the thirty-six KIAs the detachment had suffered. Now, as he turned to look around the bunker, Falconi knew this next mission was so dangerous that the Black Eagle Role of Honor would have at least three or four more names added to its roster.

Top Gordon came down the steps and stood by his commander. "As the old saying goes, sir, 'All present and accounted for.' "

"Thanks, Top," Falconi said.

Top sensed the colonel's mood. "They're a damned good bunch."

"You bet," Falconi agreed.

"They can take care of themselves, sir," Top added.

"This mission has more uncertainties than we've ever faced, Top," Falconi reminded him. "We don't even know what the target area is like."

Top thought of the need for a good scout. "That goddamned Archie!" he cursed.

"These things can't depend on one man," Falconi reminded him.

Swift Elk came into the room. He'd heard Falconi's last remark. "It's a weak link in our chain, sir. We don't have anyone to match Archie's tracking skills."

Now Fagin, who had been visiting the latrine, joined them. As usual, he had the time element foremost in his mind. He looked at his watch. "What the hell are we waiting for?"

"Not a goddamned thing," Falconi said. "We're all in a big hurry to die, Fagin. Too bad you're not coming with us."

Top Gordon didn't want the two to get into any arguments in front of the men. He quickly stepped to the front of the room. "Gentlemen!" he announced loudly. "Whippo your bloodshot eyes up here and feast 'em on our commanding officer."

Falconi stepped forward to open the briefing. Operation Dien Bien Phu Encore had now officially begun.

Chapter Five

Although Falconi's listeners were certainly military, they were not arranged in an orderly fashion as they waited for him to begin the briefing. The few folding chairs that were available were scattered haphazardly around the room. Those without them either situated themselves comfortably on the hospital beds that the enterprising supply sergeant Hank Valverde had gotten for the detachment, or lined the two walls of the bunker's main room. Ray Swift Elk, the brand-new officer, stood in the rear of the crowd. Despite the casual atmosphere, the men were most soldierly in the way they gave their commanding officer their undivided and complete attention.

"Men," Falconi said. "We're going to embark on another of our—" He paused and smiled. "—great adventures. This time, for a change, the planning is as complete as possible. But, as always, not all the information is available to us. I want you to all understand that."

Calvin Culpepper displayed a lazy grin. "I hope we

at least know *what* we're supposed to do."

"Yes we do, Calvin," Falconi said. "And we also know to *whom*. But there's a few details in between that we'll have to find out on our own. For example, we're not really sure about the exact *where* of the target."

Paulo Garcia lit a cigarette. "I thought that damned OPLAN that Fagin brought in was a bit sketchy."

"Enough bullshit," Falconi said. "Let's get down to the nitty-gritty. Our mission is to infiltrate North Vietnam in the vicinity of Dien Bien Phu. We are to locate and destroy a satellite-communications-interference complex located somewhere in the area. That's it in a nutshell. For more details, I'll let Sergeant Major Gordon carry on the briefing with the execution phase." He left the front of the room and walked toward his office motioning to Swift Elk to follow him. As usual, the two officers had plenty of last-minute details to tend to. With everyone occupied at the briefing, they could count on at least a few uninterrupted moments.

Gordon, as tough and beefy as always, took the colonel's place at the front of the room. He made note of the time. "It is now 1700. In exactly twenty-four hours we will board a C-130 aircraft on the Camp Nui Dep airstrip for an airplane ride to the operational area. Upon arrival over the drop zone—timed to be at dusk—we will exit the aircraft via static-line T10 parachutes at an altitude of 800 feet."

"Eight hundred feet!" Blue Richards exclaimed. "Hell, we won't have time enough to deploy reserves if the main chute malfunctions."

62

"That's right," Top agreed. Then he added, with a typical senior NCO scowl, "But you'll wear 'em just the same because that's what the regs call for."

Blue shook his head. "Shee-yut!"

"Now that the intellectual portion of the audience has graced us with his wit and opinion, I shall continue," Top said. "Upon arrival on the drop zone, we will be met by our asset, who will lead us to the area where a permanent base camp will be utilized for the operation."

Malpractice McCorckel raised his hand. "Who's the asset, Top?"

"Paulo will cover that in the intelligence portion," Top announced. "Once we have established ourselves in the base camp, we'll start reconnaissance patrols to acquaint us with the area and to find the Red commo station we're looking for. Once that is done, final plans will be made for the destruction of the target and the exfiltration back to friendly territory. Any questions?"

"Do we have any idea how far that station will be from our base camp?" Hank Valverde asked.

"I'm afraid not," Top answered. "We'll find out by running recon patrols."

"We could really use Archie Dobbs on this one," Blue Richards said. "He's the best damn tracker and compass man around."

"The boy has done us wrong," Calvin Culpepper said. "No doubt about it."

"There's no sense in going on about that fucking Archie," Top snapped. "I'll deal with the sonofabitch in my own way when the time comes." He paused and controlled his hot temper, which had started to

63

boil with thoughts of the AWOL scout. "Okay. Now hear this—as the Navy guys say—you'll be able to consume all the beer you want tonight, but the cutoff period will be at 0200 hours. I want you guys to get plenty of sleep. I'm holding off first call until 1000 hours tomorrow. That'll get you plenty of sacktime, and still leave several hours to tend to last-minute chores. We'll fall out of the bunker, fully equipped and loaded, at 1500. We'll go to the airstrip and draw chutes at 1515. Station time is 1545, and takeoff will be at 1600 like I've already told you. I'm afraid that's sketchy guys, but it's all I've got. If there's no questions, Paulo will give you the intelligence portion of the briefing."

Paulo ambled up to the front of the room. He didn't mince words. "We're jumping into the middle of a heavy concentration of veteran regular NVA troops."

Salty O'Rourke laughed. "Now what's the bad news?"

Paulo grinned. "The bad news is that the bastards are armed. Now for the good news. We have an asset, as Top told you. This asset is fully checked out. In fact, some of you old sweats know her."

"*Her?*" a chorus of voices called out.

"Yeah," Paulo said. "Her name is Andrea Thuy."

"We heard she was outta ops and in the States going to college," Malpractice said.

"Yeah!" Calvin added. "What the hell is she doing in North Vietnam?"

"Waiting for us, guys," Paulo said. "Andrea was born and raised in that same area. She's been quickly called in and infiltrated just for this particular problem. The lady is well set up and ready to roll. Since our operation is going to be a whiz-bang attention-getter, Andrea will be exfiltrating with us."

"Hey!" Dean Fotopoulus called out. "Is she good-looking?"

"Cool it, Romeo," Malpractice said coolly. "She and the colonel are an item."

"Sorry," Dean said. "I ain't in the know."

"You are now, ol' buddy," Calvin Culpepper said.

"At any rate," Paulo said, "we'll be in the midst of plenty of NVA. That means convoys, military posts, patrols, and all sorts of activity. The slightest carelessness, or bad luck, and we're compromised."

"What's the terrain like?" Doc Robichaux asked.

"Mountainous, mostly," Paulo replied. "Dien Bien Phu is on a plain surrounded by high ground. I'm sure all you guys realize the significance of the place. That was where the Red General Giap defeated the French garrison and brought about France's withdrawal from Indochina."

"Sure we know," Dwayne Simpson said. "It's a famous place."

"Right," Paulo said. "And that brings out one other interesting item I want to tell you about. Dien Bien Phu, good buddies, is a Communist tourist attraction. They have tours going there all the time. They've even gone so far as to reconstruct the area as it appeared at the height of the fighting. The airstrip is there, the bunkers—everything but French paras and legionnaires."

"Jesus Christ!" Jesse Makalue complained. "Why don't we just run this frigging operation in downtown Moscow?"

"It's going to be about that bad," Paulo said. "So again, let me emphasize that care and caution will be our bywords out there."

"What about the drop zone?" Gunnar Olson asked. "Will the Commies be selling ringside seats to our jump?"

"The DZ has been especially selected by Andrea Thuy," Paulo said. "It is out of sight of populated areas and roads. The jump-in at dusk will also help too." He took a deep breath. "That's the end of the intelligence briefing. Hank Valverde will give you the supply poop."

Hank was the hardest-working man in the detachment. His job as supply sergeant demanded long hours and great attention to detail. He was responsible for all items—ammo, rations, uniforms, special gear, demolitions—everything. During the preparations for missions, he was constantly running back and forth between the Black Eagle bunker and the camp's S4 as he requisitioned, drew, and issued the many items necessary to run the operation. Now, with his work winding down, he appeared tired and drawn. His customary pencil was stuck behind his ear and his ever-present clipboard, well-used and worn, was in his hands. "Okay," he said wearily. "We'll be carrying in twenty pounds of C4 explosive complete with detonators and fuses. Naturally I'm going to spread this stuff around. If one guy had it all and landed funny he'd look like a goddamned fireworks display over Coney Island. Since Blue is the main demo guy, he'll carry the plastic. Salty will tote the detonators and Top has agreed to take the fuses. I want it all to be in the demo guy's team, but since

Malpractice has the medical bag, Top agreed to relieve him of any extra burden." Hank grinned. "So if Top's Terrors land too close and hard, they're going to go up in one big swoosh!"

"Very, very funny," Top said dryly.

"Yeah," Hank said. "Okay. We'll go with the SOP loads of ammo for the weapons and that will also go for all the other gear too. There'll be nothing exotic here. Gunnar and Tiny will have an M60 to man, but they'll take in everything they need themselves."

"I'm real glad that Gunnar and Tiny ain't gonna be any trouble for the rest of us," Calvin Culpepper said, standing up. "But, hey, Hank. What if we decide we need something we didn't jump in with?"

"There will be one — I say again — *one* resupply drop available to us whenever we request it," Hank explained. "The brass figure that a single resupply will be all that can be risked due to the heavy concentration of enemy troops. So we'll have to make it count when and if we need it. Any more questions regarding supply? Okay, Sparks Johnson will give you the commo portion."

Hank left the room on some logistical errand as the new communications chief went to the front of the room. "I don't know what kind of equipment is in the base camp but it must be powerful," Sparks said. "I understand this here Andrea broad, er, lady, can talk to Saigon if she wants. The detachment has the Prick-Sixes that it's always had, so they tell me, but there'll be a new set of call signs since there's now one more team than usual. The Command Element will be Eagle. Ray's Roughnecks will be Eagle One; Top's Terrors, Eagle Two; and Calvin's Crapshooters,

Eagle Three. If there's any sub-units or details created, like patrols, they'll be Eagle Four, Five, and so on as needed."

"Hey, Sparks," Doc Robichaux said. "What'll we do with the radio gear during exfiltration? Paulo said the woman would be going with us."

"It is going to be destroyed," Sparks said. "Commo equipment that powerful will be too big and heavy to lug out, and we don't want the Reds to get their mitts on it." He looked around the room. "Any more questions? Okay. Malpractice will give you the word on medical stuff."

Malpractice seemed fresh and enthusiastic. The administrative furlough and subsequent marriage had charged his emotional batteries. Although deeply in love with his new bride, he still had a strong fatherly feeling toward the Black Eagles. "I don't have much to say," he said. Then he grinned. "There won't be any rotten women out there for you idiots to screw, so I don't have to preach about VD for a change. But I do want to emphasize that you—"

"—use water purification tablets!" Blue Richards yelled out.

Calvin laughed. "Yeah! You always say that, Malpractice."

"Just make sure you take advantage of 'em," Malpractice insisted. "Also, bring any cuts and scrapes—no matter how minor—to me for treatment. You know how easy it is to get infections out there. And if I ain't there, see Doc Robichaux. Don't forget he's a qualified medic too."

"Corpsman!" Doc corrected him. "I'm a *corpsman!*"

"Whatever," Malpractice said with a shrug.

"What about medevac?" Dwayne Simpson asked.

"That's left hanging, I'm afraid," Malpractice said. "It all depends on the exfiltration. The way we get outta there is gonna be the way we get the wounded out. In the meantime, I'll have to take damned good care of any seriously injured personnel."

Top Gordon, from the back of the room, spoke out in a loud, booming voice. "I can personally attest to Malpractice's skill. He dug a slug out of me on the Song Cai and here I am to bring scalding pee all over you guys as good as new."

"Thanks a lot, Malpractice!" Calvin Culpepper said in mock sarcasm.

"Okay, wiseguys, I'm finished," Malpractice said. "So I'll turn this grand affair back to the guy whose ass I saved—Sergeant Major Top Gordon."

"Are there any questions whatsoever?" Top asked. "About any portion of this briefing?" He scowled at the men. "If any of you jokers are unsure about anything, speak up now. The slightest ignorance on your part could cost your life or someone else's. This ain't a training exercise. All fun and games are over with now."

The roomful of men answered the question with the silence and the steady gaze of their eyes into those of their sergeant major.

Top nodded. "Okay, that's that. Now enjoy your beer."

"I guess we'd better," said Calvin Culpepper struggling to his feet. "Lord knows it might be our last."

Chapter Six

The C-130, its engines' roar changing with the extra bite of the propellers into the heavy tropical air, went into steep turn as the pilot lined up his big aircraft on the proper azimuth for the approach onto the drop zone. The airplane vibrated with the effort as the forces of the maneuver worked against the metal skin of the flying machine.

Lt. Col. Robert Falconi, standing in the door, had to hold on tightly to keep from falling back inside and across the fuselage as the horizon outside tilted sharply in relation to the airplane's attitude. Ray Swift Elk, on the other side, also braced himself against the door frames, but his problem was just the opposite of his commanding officer's. The husky Sioux had to keep from falling *out* of the C-130.

Paulo Garcia, in position behind him in the stick of jumpers, grinned and leaned forward so he could speak in the lieutenant's ear. "Hang on, sir, or you're gonna beat the rest of us into the mission!"

Swift Elk had no chance to reply. His arms now

quivered with the effort of keeping his own 180 pounds plus another 110 of parachute and equipment, from slipping into the sky outside. Although his static line was hooked up and his chute would deploy, the idea of falling short of the drop zone was not particularly appealing. There was a whole goddamned North Vietnamese army down there somewhere—not to mention a population heavily propagandized to hate Americans by its Communist Government.

The others in the detachment were jammed up against each other in anticipation of making a quick exit. The drop zone was a short one. That meant there would not be even one extra precious second to waste in "unassing" the aircraft so that all the men could hit the DZ. If the jump came off too slow, the last two or three jumpers would end up slamming into the tall trees that surrounded the area.

All jump commands had been given. The red lights glowed in the door, plainly visible to everyone in the rapidly falling dusk of the tropical evening. The men's eyes were instinctively turned toward the bulbs. Things would happen fast when they went out and the green ones came on.

Falconi leaned out the aircraft and felt the strong, continuous blast off the props in his face. He peered downward at the ground. After a few seconds he could barely perceive the drop zone ahead. At that distance it appeared as a blurry break on the horizon.

The detachment commander pulled himself back inside. He raised his thumb high to let the others know that the time for the jump was close at hand. Then he turned back to tense his body for a vigorous

71

exit.

The green light suddenly came on.

Still in that crouch, Falconi sprang up and out with every bit of strength his muscular legs could muster. He hit the prop blast outside like it was a brick wall and felt himself being pushed by the man-made hurricane off the propellers. The suspension lines were pulled from their stowage loops as the big T10 parachute deployed above him. Falconi caught a quick glimpse of a couple of the other guys in the air, then the canopy swooshed open with life and he swung under it.

He only had time to take a quick glance upward to check the chute and look down again before he came in for a rough landing. A jump altitude of 800 feet does not provide much of a ride to *terra firma*.

Falconi was fortunate the ground was soft as he made a rather respectable PLF—Parachute Landing Fall—despite the unexpected meeting with the ground.

Falconi struggled to his feet and stared down at the far end of the drop zone. He relaxed emotionally when he saw that the last men in the two sticks had managed to miss the trees and hit the extremely short drop zone.

He struck the quick-release box on the parachute harness and immediately felt relief as the weight of his gear fell from his shoulders. He quickly retrieved his M16 and cranked a round into the chamber. Shadowy figures appeared from the woods in the darkening atmosphere. Falconi did not stand on ceremony. He aimed the rifle at the nearest one.

"Ong muon goi ai?" he asked issuing the challenge

in Vietnamese.

The man, who carried an AK47 slung over his right shoulder, held out his hands in a gesture of peace. He correctly answered, *"Trung-Ta!"*

"Okay," Falconi said lowering his weapon. "We've got to get this DZ sterilized."

"You bet," the Vietnamese said. He helped Falconi gather up his gear and lug it off the drop zone. When they reached the tree line, Falconi noted that several holes had already been dug by the small reception committee. These freedom fighters had not wasted their time while waiting for the arrival of the aircraft. Falconi watched as the man threw the parachute into one of the excavations.

"Here's another," Ray Swift Elk said, showing up to bury his own.

"Did everyone make it down okay?" Falconi asked.

"Yes, sir," Swift Elk answered. "I just checked with Top. He gave me his usual 'All present and accounted for.' "

Falconi pulled out a cigarette. It would soon be too dark to smoke safely. The glow of even a single cigarette could be seen for more than a mile in the deep darkness of the tropical night. He lit up and inhaled deeply. Falconi always enjoyed that first taste of tobacco after a jump.

A feminine voice spoke out from a little farther inside the forest. "I thought you were going to give those up, Robert."

Falconi lifted his eyes — and his heart turned over.

Andrea Thuy, wearing tiger-stripe fatigues and a Vietnamese conical hat, was as beautiful as ever despite her martial appearance. The faultless blend-

73

ing of Europe and Asia in her face was like a lovely painting. She walked up to him and stopped. Then, standing on her tiptoes, she kissed him lightly on the mouth. "Aren't you even going to say hello, Robert?"

Falconi's face remained passive. He knew he still loved her with all his soul and being.

Archie Dobbs slowly lifted his head and peered over the tailgate of the deuce-and-a-half truck. He could see the motor pool awash in the weak yellow glare of the firelights as his gaze swept the area.

There were no other people around. All the vehicles were parked in their proper places, their square military design making them appear slightly foreboding. Archie climbed out of the back of the truck and dropped lightly to the ground. He'd spotted the dispatcher's shack a hundred or so meters ahead. He knew there would be someone inside, but hoped the guy would be sleepily inattentive to his duties so it would be easier to sneak out of the gate and onto the Long Binh garrison without attracting attention.

Archie had just completed one hell of a difficult trip. He'd begun by sneaking out of the Black Eagle bunker back at Camp Nui Dep and going across the garrison area to steal aboard an H34 chopper that had just brought in a load of supplies for Maj. Rory Riley's Special Forces detachment.

He'd hoped the helicopter was going to Long Binh, his destination, but instead found himself at Peterson Field. This meant he had to figure a way to get across the area and into the part of the garrison where his sweetheart Betty Lou was stationed.

Constant thoughts of this young woman filled his mind with bitterness. Archie Dobbs had never been in love before in his life. And like most guys in that predicament, when he did fall, he did it all the way. He loved 2nd Lieutenant Betty Lou Pemberton. He loved her to such an extent that he'd passed up some damned good-looking pussy in a faraway Laotian mountain fortress called Faroucheville. Archie had gotten horny as hell, just like the others, but the pure affection he had for his girlfriend had been an inspiration to him, and given him the moral strength to control his natural physical urges. But when he'd returned from the operation, instead of finding a true-blue sweetheart, he'd been handed a "Dear John" letter, in which Betty Lou had informed him she'd fallen for another guy.

Archie was an impetuous son of a bitch, and he'd taken off without thinking or planning ahead. He really didn't know what he was going to do when he found Betty Lou. It would be natural to try and win back her affections, but if he couldn't? Maybe whip her boyfriend's ass—or her's. He didn't know for sure what he'd do, but whatever it was, he would do it with the traditional Dobbs style. The gesture would be magnificent!

Now he glided among the vehicles as he silently worked his way toward the gate of the motor pool. Archie's mind worked fast as he moved along. He'd be going into officer country, and that might present a problem. As he mentally wrestled with that troublesome question, Archie came alongside the dispatch shack.

He stopped and looked around. The moment he

was about to begin his wild dash for the gate, he heard voices.

"Okay, Jenkins, I've got to roll now. Just be sure the drivers get the topped-off vehicles in the morning."

"Yes, sir."

Archie, who was behind a jeep, cautiously rose up to take a look. He saw a sergeant and an officer inside the place. They were evidently making certain things were ready for a convoy early the next day.

"I'll go check them tanks now, sir," the sergeant said. "That way we'll both sleep easier tonight, Lieutenant Braden."

"Good idea," the officer said. "I'm going to change clothes and go see the Big Man to fulfill my social obligations this evening. There's a silly-assed reception with some visiting politicos from the States. At any rate, I'll see you at the crack of dawn." The man walked away from the shack toward the gate.

Archie noted the guy's name, plus one other important thing: Lt. Braden was about his own size.

His eyes whipped around as the sergeant stepped out of the shack to stroll down the line of waiting trucks. Archie waited a couple of beats, then stole up to the little building. After one more quick look around, he reached inside and deftly removed one of the clipboards hanging on the wall by the door. Then he hurried out the gate to follow Lt. Braden back to his quarters.

Archie was thankful the walk back to the BOQ—Bachelor Officers Quarters—was a short one. He watched the lieutenant go inside, then moved into the shadows of a nondescript building across the street from the place.

Three-quarters of an hour later, showered and shaved, the lieutenant emerged and hurried off down the street. Archie waited for the officer to get a good distance away. Then he tucked the clipboard under his arm and boldly strode up to the BOQ. He stepped inside and walked up to the first room and banged loudly on the door.

An irritated officer, wearing only his shorts and shower shoes, opened up. He glared at Archie, obviously an enlisted man, with a great deal of distaste. "Well? What the hell do *you* want?"

Archie displayed the clipboard bearing the motor pool documents on it. He put a tone of pleading in his voice. "I gotta find Lieutenant Braden, sir," he said. "He forgot this here manifest for tomorrow's convoy and he's gonna need it first thing in the morning."

"Oh, hell," the irritated officer said. He pointed down the hall. "Braden is down that way, on the right side. His name is on the door."

"Gee, sir! Thanks a lot!" Archie said. He hurried away, quickly reading the stenciled letters on the doors. When he reached Braden's, he pulled out the commo knife he always carried. Quickly folding out the screwdriver part, he inserted it under the hasp on the lock and twisted.

Seconds later he was inside Braden's room. A thorough search produced a class "A" khaki uniform among the fatigues hanging there. Archie slipped into it glad that the Asian weather allowed him to skip the necktie per special regulations. He expertly bundled up his own clothing before going to the window. After making sure the coast was clear, he slipped through the opening and stepped outside. The final chore, before seeking out Betty Lou, was to stash his stuff beneath the building across the street.

After that was done, Archie set out on his search for his true love.

Andrea Thuy sat on the floor of the shack and looked across the low table at her companions. Two of them, Ray Swift Elk and Top Gordon, were old friends. The other was a former lover.

"Before we get down to business," Andrea said, "tell me about the old sweats. I saw Malpractice and Calvin, of course. But what about Kim?" She laughed. "I remember how fond he was of his grenade launcher. And Tripper, that cantankerous old horse thief."

"They bought the farm," Falconi said coldly.

Andrea lowered her eyes. "I should have known." She displayed a sad smile. "It's a rough life."

"It sure as hell is," Falconi said irritated. Then he added, "I thought you were back in the States—going to college."

Top cleared his throat and stood up. "Well, I guess I'll go check on the men." The last thing the sergeant major wanted was to get caught in a lovers' quarrel between Falconi and Andrea.

Swift Elk quickly followed his example. "Uh, yeah, Top. Mind if I join you?"

"Glad to have your company," Top said.

Falconi, feeling terribly awkward, did not want them to leave. "Stick around, guys," he said with forced cheerfulness. "This is like a class reunion."

"That's okay, sir," Top said. "We'll talk later, okay?" He nodded a good-bye, then made a quick exit. Swift Elk was on his heels.

Andrea reached across the table and took the pack of cigarettes out of Falconi's jacket pocket. "May I?"

"I didn't think you were much of a smoker," Falconi said.

"I don't inhale," she confessed. "But it gives me something to do with my hands during awkward moments."

Falconi helped her light up, then treated himself to one too. "Who were the guys on the reception committee?"

"Three operatives the Agency provided for me," Andrea replied. "They've already gone back to their original assignments. We won't be seeing them again."

"They seemed to know their business," Falconi said. "There were already holes dug for hiding the chutes and—" He stopped speaking and looked at her. "This is awkward, huh?"

Andrea sighed angrily. "Oh, shit, Robert! Let's knock it off. We've got a hell of a job to do here. Let's forget the past and get on with it. Okay?"

"Okay," Falconi said, with the past very strong and painful in his memory.

Chapter Seven

Andrea Thuy had once been a first lieutenant in the South Vietnamese army. She was a beautiful Eurasian woman in her mid-twenties. Five feet, six inches tall, she was svelte and trim, yet had large breasts and shapely hips and thighs that rounded out even her field uniforms with a provocative shape.

Andrea was born in a village west of Hanoi in the late 1940s. Her father, Doctor Gaston Roget, was a lay missionary physician for the Catholic Church. Deeply devoted to his native patients, the man served a large area of northern French Indochina in a dedicated, unselfish manner. The MD did not stint a bit in the giving of himself and his professional talents.

He met Andrea's mother just after the young Vietnamese woman had completed her nurse's training in Hanoi. Despite the difference in their races and ages — the doctor by then was forty-eight years old — the two fell in love and were married. This blending of East and West produced a most beautiful child, young Andrea Roget.

Andrea's life was one of happiness. The village where she lived was devoted to *Bac-Si* Gaston, as they called her father, and this respect was passed on to the man's wife and child. When the first hint of a Communist uprising brushed across the land, the good people of this hamlet rejected it out of hand. The propaganda the Reds vomited out did not fit when applied to the case of the gentle French doctor who devoted his time to looking after them. Besides, in that remote rural area, the Colonial Government was a faraway, unknown thing they never saw or heard from. It seemed to the villagers that it was unimportant who governed Indochina, as long as the politicians left them in peace.

Despite all this, the fanatical Communist movement could not ignore even this subtle repudiation of their ideals. Therefore, the local Red guerilla unit made a call on the people who would not follow the political philosophy they taught. To make the matter even more insidious, these agents of Soviet imperialism had hidden the true aims of their organization behind the trappings of a so-called independence movement. Many freedom-loving Indochinese fervently wanted the French out of their country so they could enjoy the fruits of self-government. They were among the first to fall for the trickery of the Communist revolution.

When the Red Viet Minh came to the village, they had no intentions of devoting the visit to pacification or even to winning the hearts and minds of the populace. They had come to make examples of those that had rejected them.

They had come to kill and destroy.

Little Andrea Roget was only three years old at the time, but she always remembered the rapine and slaughter the Red soldiers inflicted on the innocent people. Disturbing dreams and nightmares would bring back the horrible incident even in her adulthood, and the girl would recall the day with horror and revulsion.

The first people to die were *Docteur* and *Madame* Roget. Of all examples to be made, this was the most important for the murderers. The unfortunate couple was shot down before their infant daughter's eyes, and the little girl could barely comprehend what had happened to her parents. Then the slaughter was turned on the village men. Executed in groups, the piles of dead grew around the huts.

The it was the women's turn for their specific lesson in Viet Minh mercy and justice.

Hours of rape and torture went on before the females were herded together in one large group. The Soviet burp guns chattered like squawking birds of death as swarms of steel-jacketed 7.63-millimeter slugs slammed into living flesh.

Afterward, the village was burned while the wounded who had survived the first fusillades were flung screaming into the flames. When they tried to climb out of the inferno, they met the bayonets of the "liberators" of Indochina.

Finally, after this last outrage, the Communist soldiery marched off singing the songs of their revolution.

It was several hours after the carnage that the French colonial paratroopers showed up. They had received word of the crime from a young man who lived in a nearby village. He had come to see Doctor Roget for treatment of an ulcerated leg. After the youth had heard the shooting while approaching the hamlet, he'd left the main trail and approached in the cover offered by the jungle. Peering through the dense foliage, the young Indochinese had perceived the horror. Hoping to save as many as he could, or at least get the Red gangsters captured, he had limped painfully on his bad leg fifty kilometers to the nearest military post, where a company of French colonial paras were garrisoned.

The paratroopers, when they arrived, were shocked. These combat veterans had seen atrocities before. They had endured having their own people taken hostage to be executed by the Gestapo during the recent war in Europe. But the savagery of the massacre of this inconsequential little village was of such magnitude they could scarcely believe their eyes.

The commanding officer looked around at the devastation and shook his head. *"Mon Dieu! Le SS peut prendre une lecon des cettes betes!"* ("The SS could take a lesson from these beasts!")

The French colonial paras searched through the smoking ruins, pulling out the charred corpses for decent burial. One grizzled trooper, his face covered with three days' growth of beard, stumbled across little Andrea, who had miraculously been overlooked during the murderous binge of the Viet Minh. He knelt down beside her, his tenderest feelings brought to the surface by the sight of the pathetic, beautiful child. He gently stroked her cheek, then took her in his brawny arms and stood up.

"Oh, *pauvre enfante*," he cooed at her. "We will take you away from all this *horreur*." The paratroopers carried the little girl through the ravaged village to the road, where a convoy of secondhand U.S. Army trucks waited. These vehicles, barely usable, were kept running through the desperate inventiveness of mechanics who had only the barest essentials in the way of tools and parts. But, for the French who fought this thankless war, that was only par for the course.

Little Andrea sat in the lap of the commanding officer during the tedious trip into Hanoi. The column had to halt periodically to check the road ahead for mines. There was also an ambush by the Viet Minh in which the child was hidden in a ditch while the short but fierce battle was fought, until the attackers broke off and snuck away.

Upon arriving in Hanoi, the paras followed the usual procedure for war orphans and turned the girl over to a Catholic orphanage. This institution, run by the *Soeurs de la Charite* — the Sisters of Charity — did its best to check out Andrea's background. But all the records in the home village had been destroyed, and the child could say only her first name. She hadn't quite learned her last name, so all that could be garnered from her baby talk was the name "Andrea." She had inherited most of her looks from her mother, hence she was decidedly Oriental in appearance. The nuns did not know the girl had French blood. Thus Andrea Roget was given a Vietnamese name and became listed officially as Andrea Thuy.

Her remaining childhood at the orphanage was

happy. She pushed the horrible memories back into her subconscious, concentrating on her new life. Andrea grew tall and beautiful, getting an excellent education and also learning responsibility and leadership. Parentless children were constantly showing up at the orphanage. Andrea, when she reached her teens, did her part in taking care of them. This important task was expanded from the normal care and feeding of the children to teaching school. Andrea had been chosen for this extra responsibility because she was a brilliant student. The nuns, even then, were working on plans to send her to France, where she would undoubtedly earn a university degree.

But Dien Bien Phu fell in 1954.

Once again, the war had touched her life with insidious cruelty. The orphanage in Hanoi had to be closed when that city became part of the newly created nation of Communist North Vietnam. The gentle *Soeurs de la Charite* took their charges and moved south to organize a new orphanage in Attopeu, Laos.

Then the Pathet Lao came.

These zealots made the Viet Minh look like Sunday school teachers. Wild, fanatical, and uncivilized, these devotees of Marxism knew no limits in their war-making. Capable of unspeakable cruelty and displaying incredible savagery and stupidity, they were so terrible that they won not one convert in any of the areas they conquered.

Andrea was fifteen years old when the orphanage was raided. This time there was no chance for her to be overlooked or considered too inconsequential for torment. She, like all the older girls and nuns, was ravished countless times in the screaming orgy. When the rapine finally ended, the Pathet Lao set the mission's buildings on fire. But this wasn't the end of their "fun."

The nuns, because they were Europeans, were murdered. Naked, raped, and shamed, the pitiable women were flung alive into the flames. This same outrage, committed by the Viet Minh in her old village, awakened the memory of the terrible event for Andrea. She went into shock as the murder of the nuns continued.

Some screamed, but most prayed, as they endured their horrible deaths. Andrea, whose Oriental features still overshadowed her French ancestry, was thought to be just another native orphan.

She endured one more round of rape with the other girls. Then the Pathet Lao, having scored another victory for Communism, gathered up their gear and loot to march away to the next site for their campaign of Marxist expansionism.

Andrea gathered the surviving children around her. With the nuns now gone, she was the leader of their pathetic group. Instinct told her to move south. To the north were the Red marauders and their homeland. Whatever lay in the opposite direction had to be better. She could barely remember the gruff kindness of the French paratroopers, but she did recall they went south. Andrea didn't know if these same men would be there or not, but it was worth the effort to find out.

The journey she took the other children on was long and arduous. Short of food, the little column moved south through the jungle, eating wild fruit and other vegetation. For two weeks Andrea tended her flock, sometimes carrying a little one until her arms ached with the effort. She comforted them and soothed their fears as best she could. She kept up their hope by telling them of the kind people who awaited them at the end of the long trail.

Two weeks after leaving the orphanage, Andrea sighted a patrol of soldiers. Her first reaction was of fear and alarm, but the situation of the children by then was so desperate that she had to take a chance and contact the troops. After making sure the children had concealed themselves in the dense foliage, Andrea approached the soldiers. If they were going to rape her, she figured, they would have their fun but never know the orphans were concealed nearby. Timidly, the young girl moved out onto the trail in front of them. With her lips trembling, she bowed and spoke softly.

"*Chao ong.*"

The lead soldier, startled by her unexpected appearance, almost shot her. He relaxed a bit as he directed his friends to watch the surrounding jungle in case this was part of a diabolical Viet Cong trick. He smiled back at the girl. "*Chao co.* What can I do for you?"

Andrea swallowed nervously but felt better when she noted there was no red star insignia on his uniform. Then she launched into a spiel about the nuns, the orphanage — everything. When the other soliders approached and quite obviously meant her no harm, she breathed a quiet prayer of thanks under her breath.

She and the children were safe at last.

These troops, who were from the South Vietnamese army, took the little refugees back to their detachment commander. This young lieutenant followed standard practice for such situations and made arrangements to transport Andrea and her charges farther back to higher headquarters for interrogation and eventual relocation in a safe area.

Andrea was given a thorough interview with a South Vietnamese intelligence officer. He was pleased to learn that the girl was not only well acquainted with areas now under occupation by Communist troops but was also fluent in the Vietnamese, Laotian, and French languages. He passed this information on to other members of his headquarters staff for discussion about Andrea's potential as an agent. After a lengthy conference among themselves, it was agreed to keep her in the garrison when they sent the other orphans to Saigon.

Andrea waited there while a complete background investigation was conducted into her past life. They delved so deeply into the information available on her that each item of intelligence seemed to lead to another until they discovered the truth that she didn't even know. She was Eurasian, and her father a Frenchman — *Monsieur le Docteur* Gaston Roget.

This led to the girl being taken to an even higher-ranking officer for her final phase of questioning. He was a kindly-appearing colonel who saw to it that the girl was given her favorite cold drink — an iced Coca-Cola — before he began speaking with her.

"You have seen much of Communism, Andrea," he said. "Tell me, *ma cherie*, what is your opinion of the Viet Minh, the Viet Cong, and the Pathet Lao?"

Andrea took a sip of her drink, then pointed at the man's pistol in the holster on his hip. "Let me have your gun, *monsieur*, and I will kill every one of them."

"I am afraid that would be impossible," the colonel said. "Even a big soldier could not kill all of them by himself. But there is another way you can fight them."

Andrea, eager, leaned forward. "How, *monsieur?*"

"You have some very unusual talents and bits of knowledge, Andrea," the colonel said. "Those things, when combined with others that we could teach you, would make you a most effective fighter against the Communists."

"What could you teach me, *monsieur?*" Andrea asked.

"Well, for example, you know three languages. Would you like to learn more? Tai, Chinese, possibly English?"

"If that would help me kill Pathet Lao and Viet Cong," Andrea said, "then I would want to learn. But I don't understand how that would do anything to destroy those Red devils."

"These would be skills you could learn — along with others — that would enable you to go into their midst and do mischief and harm to them," the colonel said. "But learning these things would be difficult and unpleasant at times."

"What could be more difficult and unpleasant than what I've already been through?" Andrea asked.

"A good point," the colonel said. He recognized the maturity in the young girl and decided to speak to her as an adult. "When would you like to begin this new phase in your education, *mademoiselle?*"

"Now! Today!" Andrea cried, getting to her feet.

"I am sorry, *mademoiselle,*" the colonel said with a smile. "You will have to wait until tomorrow morning."

The next day's training was the first part of two solid years of intensified schooling. Because it would mask her true identity, South Vietnamese intelligence decided to have the young girl retain the name of Thuy—as the *Soeurs de la Charite* had named her.

Andrea acquired more languages along with the unusual skills necessary in the dangerous profession she had chosen for herself. Besides learning how to use disguises and mimic various accents and dialects, the fast-maturing girl picked up various methods to kill people. These included poisons and drugs, easily concealable weapons, and the less subtle method of blowing an adversary to bits with plastic explosive. After each long day of training, Andrea concluded her schedule by poring over books of mug shots and portraits showing the faces and identities of Communist leaders and officials up in the North.

Finally, with her deadly education completed, seventeen-year-old Andrea Thuy, *nee* Roget, went out into the cold.

During two years of operations, she assassinated four top Red bigwigs. Her devotion to their destruction was such that she was even willing to use her body if it would lower their guard and aid her in gaining their confidence. Once that was done, Andrea displayed absolutely no reluctance in administering the *coup de grace* to put an end to their efforts at spreading world Communism.

When the American involvement in South Vietnam stepped up, a Central Intelligence Agency case officer named Clayton Andrews learned of this unusual young woman and her deadly talents. Andrews had been tasked with creating an elite killer/raider outfit. After learning of Andrea, he knew he wanted her to be a part of this crack team. Using his influence and talents of persuasion, he saw to it that the beautiful female operative was sent to Langley Air Force Base in Virginia, to the special CIA school located there.

When the Americans finished honing her fangs at Langley, she returned to South Vietnam and was put into another job category. Commissioned a lieutenant in the ARVN, she was appointed a temporary major and assigned to Special Operation Group's Black Eagle Detachment, which was under the command of Capt. Robert Falconi.

Andrea accompanied the Black Eagles on their first mission. This operation, named Hanoi Hellground, was a direct-action type against a Red whorehouse and pleasure palace deep within North Vietnam. Andrea participated in the deadly combat that resulted, killing her share of the Red enemy in the firefights that erupted in the green hell of the jungle. There was not a Black Eagle who would deny she had been superlative in the performance of her duties.

But she soon fell out of grace.

Not because of cowardice, sloppy work, or inefficiency, but because of that one thing that could disarm any woman — love. She went head-over-heels into it with Robert Falconi.

Clayton Andrews was promoted upstairs, and his place was taken by another CIA case officer. This one, named Chuck Fagin, found he had inherited a damned good outfit — except that its commander and one of its operatives were involved in a red-hot romance. An emotional entanglement like that spelled disaster with a capital D in the espionage and intelligence business. It was a situation that could not be tolerated.

Fagin had no choice but to pull Andrea out of active ops. He put her in his office as the administrative director. Andrea did not protest. Deep in her heart she knew that the decision was the right one. She would have done the same thing. She or Falconi might have lost their heads and done something emotional or thoughtless if either one had suddenly been placed into a dangerous situation. That sort of illogical action could have resulted, not only in their own deaths, but in the demise of other Black Eagles as well. At times a dedicated operative had to be tough on herself.

She went out into the cold twice more after that, however. Once during operations with a Chinese mercenary guerrilla unit, and again when captured by Communist agents and taken north. This final episode ended with her rescue by Falconi. When she returned to South Vietnam, she'd been sent Stateside to recuperate and be retrained.

Now, eager and mad as hell, Andrea Thuy was back to kick Commie butt.

Chapter Eight

Archie Dobbs, now dressed in the lieutenant's uniform, walked confidently up the street toward the nurses' quarters where 2nd Lieutenant Betty Lou Pemberton was billeted. His emotions, a combination of anger, anticipation, and apprehension, were barely under control. His mood did lighten a bit when the MP on the gate of barbed-wire fence surrounding the installation gave him a snappy salute.

Archie smiled. "How's it going, soldier?"

"Fine, sir," the MP replied.

"You men are doing a great job, and we appreciate it," Archie said magnanimously to this member of the Army branch he hated the most. "But I wish you'd go easier on the enlisted men when they're having a good time in town."

"Yes, sir," the MP responded with a quizzical expression on his face.

"The boys are just blowing off a bit of steam," Archie said. "Remember that, will you?"

"Yes, sir," the MP repeated.

Archie winked at him in a big-brotherly sort of way. He strolled boldly up to the front door and stepped into the tiny foyer on the other side.

A young woman from the medical corps, sporting the insignia of a specialist four, sat at a desk reading a copy of *Vogue* magazine. She glanced up at Archie and smiled. "What can I do for you, sir?"

Archie started to ask for Betty Lou when another nurse stepped into the foyer from the living quarters. Her eyes widened when she spotted the "officer."

Archie recognized her as one of Betty Lou's best friends. "Hi, Anne."

"Hello, Archie." Then she noticed his uniform. "Good Lord in Heaven! Did they—"

"Never mind," Archie hissed at her. "I'll explain later. Tell Betty Lou I want to see her."

The nurse named Anne shook her head. "She's not here in the billets, Archie. Betty Lou went over to the officers' club."

Archie sneered. "Yeah? With her boyfriend, huh?"

"What boyfriend?"

"Hey, Anne, don't bother lying, okay?" Archie said. "She sent me a 'Dear John.' I got the god-damned thing when I got back to Nui Dep from ops. That's why I'm here."

"Oh, damn!" Anne said. She hesitated, but finally spoke. "You'll have to talk to Betty Lou about that."

"I sure as hell intend to," Archie said. "Which way is that damned officers' club?"

"Come on, Archie," Anne said. "I'm on my way over there myself."

She slipped her arm through Archie's and led him

back outside. As they walked through the gate, Archie turned his head and spoke to the MP. "Don't forget what I said about them enlisted men, soldier."

"Yes, sir!"

Anne tugged at him and they stepped up the pace. She lowered her voice. "What in hell are you doing dressed up in that uniform?"

"Don't worry about it," Archie said. "I came all the way back here from Nui Dep to see her. I figured this would make it easier."

"It'll make it easier for you to end up in the stockade," Anne said.

"To hell with this uniform," Archie snapped. "Just tell me about the sonofabitch she threw me over for."

But Anne shook her head. "I told you I'd let Betty Lou explain to you all about that 'Dear John.' "

They both slipped into silence for the next ten minutes as they walked rapidly toward their destination. When they reached the officers' club, Anne suddenly stopped. "I've changed my mind," she said. "I don't want to be anywhere near you two this evening. There's too much potential for a violent scene—and I really hate violence, Archie. Especially between two people I happen to like very, very much." She pointed toward the door. "Betty Lou is in there, Archie."

"Thanks, Anne," Archie said. He waved to her as she walked away. Then he turned and approached the door. He could hear a terrible band playing in a god-awful manner as he went inside. The place was crowded with officers, nurses, good-looking Vietnamese women, and a staff of waitresses who scurried around waiting on the numerous tables packed around the dance floor.

Archie weaved his way through the crowd to an open space and surveyed the couples swaying back and forth to the music. He grimaced at the tune and looked across the club and noted that the band was a local one. The girl singer was obviously intoning her song phonetically. Archie barely recognized it as the new tune "Born Free."

The place was so packed with people he couldn't find Betty Lou. Archie decided to play it cool and suave. He sauntered to the bar and ordered a scotch-and-soda. After he was served, he took a sip and turned around to casually survey the crowd. He nodded to a captain standing beside him.

"How're you doing?" the captain said politely.

"Pretty good," Archie said with a smile. He treated himself to another slurp of the drink. "Good scotch," he remarked.

"Only the best," the captain said.

"Yeah," Archie said. "I wonder what the enlisted men are doing tonight."

The captain shrugged. "Getting drunk and laid as usual, I suppose."

"My! My!" Archie said drolly. "Ain't they quaint?"

The captain was not amused at what he considered a slam at GIs. "I spent ten years as an enlisted man."

"Oh, God!" Archie moaned. "The fucking army is getting so goddamned democratic!" He finished off the drink and clumped the glass on the bar. "I think I'll dance. See you later."

"Take your time," the captain said.

Archie thought that he would be able to find Betty Lou more easily if he circulated unnoticed around the dance floor. Doing his best to look debonair, he approached a good-looking American woman dressed in a smart civilian dress at one of the tables. He bowed and complimented her. "Lovely dress."

"Why, thank you."

"It seems strange to see a white woman not in uniform," Archie said. "At least around the club."

The woman smiled. "I'm an invited guest here. Actually I'm a journalist for a newspaper syndicate."

"How interesting," Archie said. "By the way, would you care to dance?"

"Not right now, thank you," she replied. "Later perhaps."

"That's okay," Archie replied. "I've got to go take a shit anyway." He walked away leaving the woman staring at him in open-mouthed shock and revulsion.

The Vietnamese band ended their song, and the dancers melted off the floor and flowed back to their tables. Archie walked slowly around scanning the crowd.

Then he stopped.

Betty Lou Pemberton, his true love, sat with two other nurses at a table in a far corner. Archie's heart ached with a sweet, longing agony. Betty Lou looked adorable. Her auburn hair, worn in a short style, framed her cute little face with that pert, upturned nose. A sprinkling of freckles completed the affect.

Archie fought down his sadness and changed his mood. Suddenly, with his teeth clinched in anger, he strode across the room and stopped in front of her. "Hello, Betty Lou."

"Archie!"

"Where is he, goddamnit!" Archie growled.

"Where is the sonofabitch?"

"Archie," Betty Lou said. "I —" She stared at him. "Where did you get that uniform?"

"Don't work up a sweat about it," he said.

"Archie!" she said, getting up. "You could get into a lot of trouble!"

One of the nurses smiled up at him. "Who's your friend, Betty Lou? I don't believe we've met him."

"I'll introduce you later," Betty Lou said. She grabbed Archie's hand and led him across the club and through a door to a separate dining area. It was a dark room, with candles burning on the tables.

A Vietnamese waiter, who had been trained in his profession during the days of French colonial rule, appeared out of the gloom. "A table for *monsieur et mademoiselle?*"

"Yes!" Betty Lou exclaimed. "One toward the back of the room."

"*Mais oui!* Follow me, please."

They trailed the waiter to an intimate table for two. He took an order for wine, then left them with dinner menus. Archie watched him leave, then he glared at Betty Lou. "Don't try to protect your boyfriend! I'm gonna brutalize and injurize the bastard!"

Betty Lou took a deep breath. "Oh, Archie! There is no boyfriend!"

"I got your letter, Betty Lou," Archie said. "The one you wrote that sent me to dumpsville. You said you'd found another guy and we were through."

"Archie! Archie!" Betty Lou cried. Then she quieted down as the waiter arrived with their wine.

The man opened the bottle, then properly poured

a bit into a glass and handed it to Archie to sample.

"Gimme a whole glass, goddamnit!" Archie said. "I don't drink my booze a sip at a time."

"Of course, *monsieur*," the waiter said. He raised an eyebrow, then poured them each a glassful. "Would you care to order now?"

"Hell, no," Archie said. "I'll yell for you when I'm ready, okay?"

"*Oui, monsieur*," the waiter said coldly. He left them alone after casting an aloof, totally disapproving glance at Archie.

Archie waited until he was out of earshot. "Now let's get back to our conversation. Where the hell is that puking boyfriend?"

"There is no boyfriend, Archie," Betty Lou said.

"Damn it, Betty Lou! Don't play with my feelings," Archie said. "That letter tore me up inside. It busted my heart."

"Archie!"

"You know what I done? I went AWOL—I stole this here uniform—and I want satisfaction," Archie said. "Ol' Top Gordon is gonna fry my ass before this is all over and done with. So don't start covering up."

"I'm not covering up, Archie," Betty Lou said. "There really is no other man. There never was."

Archie hung his head. "God! This is even worse. You just plain don't love me no more."

Tears welled up in Betty Lou's eyes. "I love you, Archie. I've never stopped loving you."

He felt happily relieved, but was strongly confused. "Then why'd you unload that 'Dear John' on me?"

"Oh, God," she said with a sigh. She took a sip of

her wine. "I wanted to break up with you, Archie. But it wasn't because I didn't care for you. It's just the opposite. I care for you too much."

He shook his head. "Goddamnit! Now I'm really confused. I suppose if you hated me, you'd want to run off and get married, huh?"

"Let me explain, okay?"

"Okay."

"*I'm* the one with the rival, Archie."

"Are you crazy? I ain't got any other girlfriend," Archie protested. "I even turned down pussy on account o' you!"

"That's not a very elegant way to put it," Betty Lou said. "But I do appreciate that."

"You should!" Archie said. "Anyhow, what's this about a rival?"

"I wish it were only another woman, Archie. I could handle that. But it's the Black Eagles," Betty Lou said. "You'll always go off with them and leave me behind. And my tour in Vietnam will be up in three months. Then what will we do?"

"I hadn't thought about it," Archie confessed.

"Would you transfer back to the States?" Betty Lou asked.

"I don't know," he said softly. A complete understanding of her feelings and uncertainties swept over him.

Betty Lou reached across the table and laid her hand on his. "Archie, I'm not going back there to wait for some undeterminable amount of time for you." She paused and her voice broke. "And if something happened to you out there, I might not even be able to find out about it."

"I've always leveled with you about the Black Eagles," Archie said. "Maybe I shouldn't have."

"I only thought it best that we split up and end it here and now," Betty Lou said. "A nice, clean break with some sweet memories left over."

"I'm glad to hear from you face to face," Archie said. He looked into her eyes. "I do love you, Betty Lou."

She smiled. "I know. Your being here proves that."

"Okay, honey," Archie said. "You call the shots. Maybe you know what's best. I'll do anything you want. I promise. No scenes, no big emotional blow out. We'll do it just like you want—that nice, clean break."

"I can't do it now," Betty Lou said. "I knew I wasn't strong enough to carry through with it if I saw you again."

"Let's face up to it," Archie said. "We're in love." He smiled. "Let's order that dinner."

"All right, Archie," she said. "Then what?"

"I've got to get back to the Black Eagles, I'm afraid."

Betty Lou wiped at her eyes. "I know, Archie."

Chapter Nine

Dwayne Simpson held up his hand and motioned for Ray's Roughnecks behind him to halt.

Ray Swift Elk, Paulo Garcia, and Jesse Makalue did exactly that. They silently squatted in position, then turned to cover their area of firepower responsibility. This was SOP—Standing Operational Procedure—in the Black Eagles while out on operations. Each man was assigned a specific area to cover. This practice afforded them overall security in hairy situations.

Dwayne, acting as point man for this small reconnaissance operation, went down on his belly and quietly inched forward through the heavy vegetation that had obscured his vision. It was this sudden inability to see ahead that had caused him to call their small but deadly procession to a halt.

The black man, his ebony face streaked with dark green camouflage paint, finally reached a good point where he could peer outward. He saw a series of open rice paddies spread out to his direct front.

Although unoccupied at that particular time, they would be a dangerous place for a patrol to venture. There was a hell of a good chance for a casual observer to catch sight of the patrol.

Dwayne, still on his belly, crawled backward into the jungle. He reached a point where he could stand up, and he walked back to Ray. "This area is inhabited, sir," he said. "There's paddies out there. Nobody's working 'em, but you can bet your last payday dollar that there's a village close by."

"No doubt," Swift Elk said. He spoke into his Prick-Six radio. "Eagle, this is Eagle One. Over."

Sparks Johnson's gravelly voice came over the receiver. "This is Eagle. Over."

"We're two hours into the patrol and still can't find the target area," Swift Elk said. "There's a village in this vicinity. We're going to circle around and see if there's anything on the other side. Over."

This time it was Lt. Col. Robert Falconi's voice on the air. "Roger that, Eagle One. But return to base camp within two hours. I say again. Return in two hours. Over."

"Wilco. Out," Swift Elk said. He turned off the power button on the little radio. "You heard that, Buffalo Soldier. Lead on."

"Yes, sir," Dwayne said. He liked being called "Buffalo Soldier" by the Indian officer. That's exactly what his own great-grandfather had been in the 10th United States Colored Cavalry Regiment.

The patrol turned east and moved slowly. They stopped frequently while Dwayne moved forward to the edge of the tree line to check outside the jungle for signs of the communications station they were

103

charged with destroying.

Each time, he saw nothing but rice paddies.

After an hour, Swift Elk called a break. The fire team formed the usual perimeter, and settled down to catch their breath. The Sioux leader conferred with his second-in-command, Paulo Garcia. The Marine was not optimistic about the area.

"We keep seeing the same thing," Paulo said lighting a cigarette. "I think we stumbled into a Commie rice commune or something."

"Probably," Swift Elk agreed. "There's isn't a soul in sight, which means they're probably in the communal hut having meetings on how to increase production."

Paulo took a deep, satisfying drag of the smoke. "Yeah. That's a regimented population out there, all right. It has to be, or there'd be one or two individualistic bastards working those paddies."

Swift Elk pulled his map from the large pockets on the side of his trousers. He unfolded it and studied the document. "This thing is so fucking outdated the French couldn't have used it," he complained.

Dwayne Simpson bit off a chaw of his favorite brand of chewing tobacco. "Poor folks like us got to make do with what the good Lord give us."

"Listen to that shit. Humble country-boy philosophy from a guy who was raised on Army posts," Swift Elk said, displaying a pseudo-scowl at him. "Anyhow, poor folks like *us* got to make do with what the good Falconi gives us."

Jesse checked his watch. "We got time for another quick look-around before we head back to the base camp."

"Right," Swift Elk said. "So let's make the most of it." He stood up. "Let's check out the possibility of any jungle trails around here. The place may be hidden somewhere under this thick canopy of trees."

Dwayne and the others also stood up. The point man treated himself to a quick drink of the lukewarm water in his canteen. "Let's move out, gentlemen," he said making a mock bow. "Walk this way, please."

The going was rough through the thick vegetation. Vines, stickers, and branches held up the patrol as they moved forward in search of their objective. The plant life seemed to have a mind of its own as it grabbed at clothing and scratched exposed areas of skin.

Dwayne, in the lead, could not see more than five feet in front of him. Most of the time his vision was cut to a yard or two. He stepped easily, not letting his full weight down until he was sure the ground beneath was firm. He was also concerned about stepping on dry twigs or kicking loose rocks and making unnecessary noise.

Yet, despite these precautions, the situation went to hell.

Dwayne attempted to ease through a stand of thick bamboo when suddenly the plants gave way. He stumbled forward and fell face first out onto a well-worn trail.

The NVA soldier ten meters away was as startled as Dwayne—but he wasn't as fast.

Dwayne brought up his M16 and flipped off the safety in one movement. A couple of quick squeezes on the trigger sent an equal number of bullets streaking outward to punch into the Red trooper. The guy's fist instinctively tightened, and his AK47 sprayed out a half dozen slugs straight up into the tropical sky.

Dwayne crashed back into the bamboo and rushed toward the patrol. "Bandits back there. I got one," he announced to Swift Elk. "But I think he's got friends."

That was quickly confirmed when several volleys of shots smacked into the vegetation around them. Ray's Roughnecks, well-practiced in battle drill from workouts together back in Camp Nui Dep, responded in kind. A couple of screams gave evidence of their accuracy.

"Make some noise!" Swift Elk yelled to his three men. "I want them bastards to think we're hauling ass all the way back to Sioux Falls."

The team crashed back into the jungle sounding more like four trucks than a quartet of skilled jungle fighters. Then Swift Elk signaled a halt. Using hand and arm signals, he silently ordered his men into firing positions.

There were no sounds for a full five minutes. The surrounding jungle was eerie in its silence. But it was a quietness that screamed with danger. When no insects flew nor birds sang, it could only mean alien presences in their midst.

Then a loud "crack" was heard as a careless foot stepped on a dead branch lying on the ground. Swift Elk and the guys tensed.

The first NVA came into view, his green uniform and pith helmet barely visible in the surrounding deep monsoon forest. Another appeared off to the side—then one more. They were obviously formed into a skirmish line of sorts.

Swift Elk, never a believer in formality, didn't bother to introduce himself. He just cut loose on full automatic. The rest of the Roughnecks did likewise, making the close atmosphere turn into a deafening, exploding hell of small-arms fire.

The NVA skirmish line, now numbering six, was blown back and down by the fussillade. Then, again, there was silence.

The battle was over.

Cautiously, at the ready, the fire team stood up and moved toward the fallen enemy. Jesse made an obvious statement. "They're all dead."

"Look at them uniforms," Paulo said. "These guys are garrison soldiers. They weren't out here on no patrol."

"You're right," Swift Elk said. "This is probably a picket post."

"Shit!" Dwayne swore. "Don't tell me they was expecting us!"

Swift Elk shook his head. "Nope. These bastards are here to make sure the peasants that work those rice paddies don't run away."

"The sonofabitches!" Jesse swore. "This area must be crawling with other guys from their outfit."

Paulo Garcia treated himself to another cigarette. "It's gonna make our job of finding that damn communications station a hell of a lot harder."

Dwayne checked his watch. "We'd better head back, boys, or we'll be late for supper."

"Move out," Swift Elk ordered. He took another look around the jungle. It seemed to him that the Black Eagle Detachment had been dealt nothing but a hand of down cards—and none of them were worth a damn for taking the pot.

Chuck Fagin tilted back in his plush, leather office chair and put his feet up on his desk. He lifted the iced glass of Irish whiskey and soda to his lips and took the first delicious sip. Then the phone in front of him rang.

"Shit!"

It rang again.

"Shit! Shit!" He put his feet down and leaned forward picking up the instrument. "Yeah?"

"Mister Fagin, this is the front gate."

"Jeez!" Fagin said. "This is the first time I ever talked to a goddamned gate. Most o' the time you fuckers just squeak when you're pushed open or pulled shut."

"Hey," the irritated MP on the other end said. "You want to listen to what I got to say or not?"

"Sorry, guy," Fagin said. "You caught me in the bath."

"There's a lieutenant down here that wants to see you," the MP said. "He ain't got the right paperwork on him. In fact, he ain't got any ID a 'tall. But he does know the password and countersign—all up to date."

"What's his name?" Fagin asked.

"Dobbs," the MP answered. "Lieutenant Archibald Dobbs."

"*Dobbs!*" Fagin bellowed. "That fucker ain't a—" He calmed down. "Please send the lieutenant up to see me," he said softly. "I'd love to visit with him."

"Awright," the MP said. "But I got to get an escort

for him."

"Oh, please hurry," Fagin said in a voice dripping with sweetness. "I am really anxious to see him."

"Okay, Mister Fagin."

Fagin hung up the telephone. He reached for the mixed drink, then hesitated. He turned from it and abruptly got up to go over to his liquor cabinet. Fagin pulled out the fifth of Irish whiskey and put the bottle to his mouth. Tilting back his head, he took several throat-searing swallows of the liquor.

"I really need that," he said to himself. "Especially with that crazy Dobbs showing up on my doorstep in an officer's uniform for Chrisssake!"

Within fifteen minutes there was a knock on the office door. Fagin opened it and looked dully out at Archie Dobbs standing there grinning with an MP escort.

"Hi ya, Chuck!"

"Hello, Lieutenant," Fagin said with a sugary smile. "How nice to see you again."

"The pleasure is mine, Chuck," Archie said stepping inside. He looked back at the MP. "Remember what I told you, young fellow. Always be kind to enlisted men when they're drunk. Their rowdiness is only an expression of youthful exuberance."

"Yes, sir!" the escort said. He saluted and executed a fancy about-face.

Fagin shut the door. "What can I do for you, asshole? And where in hell did you get that officer's getup?"

Archie grinned. "Sharp, huh?" He walked over to the large mirror mounted on the wall. "If I knew I looked this good in a lieutenant's duds, I'd have went to West Point."

"There's only one thing that kept you outta West Point, dude," Fagin said.

"What's that?" Archie asked.

"High school," Fagin replied. "They like you to have a diploma from one of 'em before they let you in as a cadet."

"Enough of this chit-chat," Archie said. "I got an obvious favor to ask o' you, Fagin."

"Oh, yeah? What's that?"

"I need a ride back to Nui Dep," Archie said. "I want my pals to see me all gussied up like this."

"No shit?" Fagin said. He walked to his chair and sat down. "Well, you AWOL sonofabitch, I got some real sad news for you. And it sure as hell oughta take the glitter off those lieutenant bars you're sporting."

"No kidding?" Archie remarked nonchalantly.

"Yeah! Your buddies ain't at Nui Dep," Fagin said. "They're on a mission in North Vietnam."

Archie's face paled. "Don't shit me about that, Fagin. It ain't funny."

"I ain't trying to be funny," Fagin said. "They've been committed for about three days now."

Archie stammered. "Well—when did this—how did this happen?"

"Same as always," Fagin said nonchalantly. "I was given an OPLAN and I took it out to them. An old sweat like you knows what happens after that. Especially when there's a real need to move quickly on a special operation."

Archie slumped down in a chair on the other side of the desk. "They can't get along without me, man! I'm their scout—their eyes and ears!"

Fagin's voice was cold. "They needed you and you weren't there, Dobbs. We couldn't give 'em the exact location of the target because we didn't know it ourselves."

"They'll get creamed!" Archie exclaimed.

"Could be," Fagin said coldly. "And if this mission goes to hell and they buy the farm because they can't find the objective, you'll never have another full night's sleep even if you live to be a hundred."

Archie, uncharacteristically, said nothing. Devastated, he simply lowered his head and stared down at the floor.

Chapter Ten

The NVA soldier stood on the jungle trail and pointed into the thick vegetation at the spot where the bamboo was broken. "They went that way, Comrade Captain!"

The captain, a young infantry officer named Truong, nodded his head in understanding. "What caused them to do this rash thing? What sort of reactionary interlopers did they discover?"

The soldier shrugged. "I do not know, Comrade Captain. I was up the trail at my post when I heard shooting. I did as we had been instructed, and immediately chambered a bullet into my weapon." He held up his Kalashnikov assault rifle. "Then I made sure no one passed my position."

"Well done, Comrade Soldier," Captain Truong said. "Did the others not call out to you? Is it possible they shouted some information that you have forgotten? Perhaps a description of their quarry?"

The soldier almost became defensive. "I would have remembered if they had, Comrade Captain. I speak the truth!"

"Of course you do," Truong said soothingly. "Now let us follow the paths of our unfortunate comrades."

"It is a most saddening sight, Comrade Captain!"

"Looking upon dead comrades is always unpleasant," Truong said.

It was ironic that the officer would make such a comment. In truth, he had never seen actual combat. By sheer chance, the captain had spent the entire three years he had been in the Army stationed in the Dien Bien Phu area. He was serving as the commander of a guard company detailed to keep the peasants from fleeing south from the communal farm where they'd been assigned by the Government. "Let us follow the path through the brush."

A veteran sergeant named Dinh, who had been silently standing off to one side, quickly stepped up. "Pardon, Comrade Captain. I think it best that we send two men ahead of us with their rifles at the ready." This NCO was a disabled veteran of heavy fighting in the South. Dinh walked with a painful limp and had been invalided to the guard company. "There still may be ambushers about the area."

Truong quickly tugged his Tokarev automatic pistol from the leather holster on his belt. "Of course, Comrade Sergeant. I was just about to issue such orders." He turned and pointed to two other soldiers. "Follow the track into the jungle. *Can-than!* Take care!"

The first soldier, an eager teenager anxious for adventure, rushed through the break in the bamboo. The other, a physically limited veteran like the sergeant, was not so enthusiastic. He swallowed hard, fearing what might be ahead, and gingerly followed his younger comrade into the brush.

It was easy to follow the broken branches and trampled vegetation along the trail that the unlucky fighters had taken. Sergeant Dinh suddenly hollered out, "Halt!"

Everyone, surprised, turned to look at him. "It is wise to stay on the alert and to keep one's eyes open," he counseled. "Even the smallest items can give one a great amount of useful information."

The non-commissioned officer bent his legs and painfully squatted down. He picked up something shiny from the ground.

"What have you found, Comrade Sergeant?" Truong asked.

"A spent cartridge," Dinh announced, studying it.

Truong frowned at this interruption in the proceedings. "Of course there are cartridges, Comrade Sergeant. We all know there was shooting, correct?"

"Yes, Comrade Captain," the sergeant said. "But this one is American. A 5.56-millimeter as used in their rifles type M16."

"Nonsense! Where would escaping peasants get such weapons?"

"Perhaps, Comrade Captain, they were not peasants," Sergeant Dinh suggested.

Truong smirked a bit, then signaled to the two soldiers leading the way. *"Tien len!* Go ahead!"

114

The small column continued forward for another ten minutes, then they suddenly halted when the young trooper ahead gasped loudly.

Now the sergeant smirked. "He has found the dead ones, Comrade Captain."

"Of course," Truong said. He gritted his teeth and forced himself go forward. When he reached the place where the bodies were, he involuntarily sucked in his breath.

The corpses, badly torn, were strewn out in undignified positions. The savagery of the swarm of bullets that had struck them down was obvious in the gaping wounds that had been blown in the flesh. Flies buzzed around them, and the jungle heat had encouraged a quick start in decomposition. Internal gasses had already swollen the bodies.

Dinh calmly strode past them and began searching the area. Finally he knelt down and again grabbed spent brass. This time it was a whole handful of cartridges. "The killers fired from here. Every shot, it appears, was on full automatic. And they set up their positions hastily, but skillfully."

"And what are we to surmise from that, Comrade Sergeant?" Truong asked feeling a bit chastened.

"These were definitely not escaping peasants," the sergeant said. "I suggest, Comrade Captain, that you contact regimental headquarters and file a full report. This will require special planning and action."

"It shall be done, Comrade Sergeant!" Truong said almost obediently.

The Rung-Ram bird twittered loudly in its irrita-

115

tion. Robert Falconi ignored the chattering and lowered the binoculars. He'd spent an entire ten minutes using the instruments to make visual sweeps across the valley below him.

Blue Richards, lying beside him on the densely overgrown mountainside, spoke in a whisper. "See anything, sir?"

"Sure," Falconi answered. "There's a farm village down there on the flatlands. But not one modern building or even a hint of an electronic surveillance operation."

"Damn!" Blue said. "We just ain't having any luck at all."

"We're having luck," Falconi contradicted him. "*Bad* luck."

"Well, them Reds must have that place perty well hid away," Blue said. "Or we'd have found it by now."

"Let's get back to the others," Falconi said.

The two eased back from their impromptu observation post, and got to their feet. They walked twenty meters deeper into the jungle until they found the rest of Top's Terrors situated in a tight, tidy defensive perimeter.

Top Gordon greeted them. "I can see by the expressions on your faces that you didn't catch sight of what we're after."

"Nope," Falconi said. "It may take some time, but we will."

"Each day that passes without action means another twenty-four hours of interference with American satellite communications," Top said.

"You don't have to remind me," Falconi said bitterly.

Malpractice McCorckel turned from his place on the perimeter. "We're gonna have to start worrying about heat stroke pretty soon, sir," he said. "The boys have been doing a hell of a lot of humping in these high temperatures."

"Yeah," Falconi agreed. "You're right. But the mission comes first. It can't be helped."

"The mission won't be pulled off if ever'body is down sick," Malpractice said. Then the medic added, "Or if two or three croak. This here weather is dangerous as hell. I swear I could boil eggs in this humidity."

"Your point is well taken, Malpractice. I can't give you any arguments," Falconi said. He'd packed two canteens with him since they'd left the base camp three hours previously, and he was nearly out of water. A heavily perspiring man needed plenty of the old H_2O to keep him going. "We'd better move back now."

Although Falconi was the commanding officer, Top was technically in charge of the patrol. It was a team mission, and the lieutenant colonel had come along at the last minute. He wanted to see for himself what the problem was with locating the target. Now he knew. It was a tiny place in a huge area.

"On your feet," Top said. "Salty, take the point."

"Aye, aye," the veteran Marine sergeant said. He moved out with Malpractice behind him. Top and Falconi took up the middle of the column while Blue Richards covered the rear.

The going in the heavily vegetated, up-and-down terrain was torturous and exhausting. The men traveled slowly and silently, gasping for breath

117

through dry mouths as the last of their water finally gave out. The experience was painful and taxing, creating a situation in which even experienced fighting men become careless and inattentive.

The explosive of AK47 fire was almost in Salty O'Rourke's face.

He jumped back instinctively and caught a brief glimpse of the NVA soldier ahead of him in the brush. Salty pumped three quick shots while moving rapidly backward.

Malpractice, as per detachment SOP, moved to cover the right side of the retreating point man while Top went to the left. They could see no one in front of them, but they fired off several salvos of 5.56-millimeter slugs just in case there might be some concealed NVA to the front.

A shriek of pain showed they'd been right.

Now more AK47 shooting exploded outward toward the Black Eagles. Falconi, actually serving as a rifleman, moved forward to take Top's place in the line as the sergeant major issued his commands.

"Blue! Move up to Salty and hold fast," Top shouted. "Ever'body! Cover the front."

It was obvious that all incoming fire was from that direction, so Top couldn't afford to have anyone uselessly guarding the rear. He wanted the fire team's bullet-power all forward toward the threat.

There were some shouted commands in Vietnamese out in the jungle. *"Tien len!"*

Falconi, fluent in the language, shouted a warning. "Here they come!"

In less than ten seconds a dozen NVA rushed toward them. Their maneuver was so precise that it had to be out of a military textbook. Dressed right as if on parade, the Red soldiers advanced at a steady pace.

Salty O'Rourke, a bit amused, pulled a grenade off his harness. After deftly removing the pin, he let the spoon pop. Then Salty tossed it hard and slightly above the level of the enemy's heads.

The explosive device did exactly what he knew it would. It zipped through the tall bushes, the leaves and branches slowing it down considerably.

Then it abruptly fell to the ground.

There was an immediate sharp explosion and the Black Eagles caught a brief glimpse of a bloodied, mangled NVA cartwheeling through the air before disappearing back into the bushes.

The guy's buddies, braver than they were smart, pressed on doggedly while maintaining their regulated and carefully spaced shooting.

Falconi and his four men waited until they came into view a bit better. Then they swept the muzzles of their M16s back and forth as if they were garden hoses.

It only took three seconds.

"Cease fire!" Top bellowed. He waited a couple of beats and could detect no more movement out to the front. "Salty! Run a quick recon about fifty meters out, then come back."

Salty acknowledged the order with a wave of his hand and moved out to tend to the task assigned him.

Malpractice quickly went to the NVA and checked them out. That didn't take long either. "All dead," he said to no one in particular.

"Blue," Falconi said. "Give the stiffs a search. Pull out any papers you can find. We'll let Paulo make an intelligence evaluation on 'em.

"Aye, aye, sir," Blue said. The job was more than a bit messy because of the blood and gore. "I wish these bastards would've died cleaner."

Malpractice grinned. "We should have got you to sing one o' your country-western songs. That would've killed 'em quick and clean."

Top laughed. "Yeah. But think o' the horrible expressions they would've had on their faces."

"You guys just don't recognize talent," Blue said as he pulled an ID document off one of the corpses. "I might leave this here man's army and go on to Nashville and get me a recording contract."

"I used to have an ol' tom cat sounded better'n you," Malpractice said.

"He was prob'ly smarter too," Top said.

Blue scowled at them as he stood up from the last corpse. "Just don't none o' y'all come callin' on me at my fancy house after I'm a big star," he warned them. Then he winked. "Unless you got good-lookin' women with you."

"Knock off the bullshit!" Falconi snapped. "What'd you find, Blue?"

"Just reg'lar ol' identification papers, sir," Blue said.

"Take 'em back to Paulo anyhow," Falconi said. "He can probably make some use of them."

Salty O'Rourke returned from his short patrol. "Them guys was at a guard post up ahead," he reported. "There ain't no more NVA around."

"If any more of the mothers heard this shooting

120

there soon will be," Falconi said. "Let's head back."

"Another wasted day," Malpractice said. "We're gonna end up being on this mission forever."

"Yeah—if we're lucky," Top added. "Because out here you generally don't live forever."

Chapter Eleven

The atmosphere at the dinner was strained. What had begun as a pleasant evening, even if the gaiety was forced a bit, deteriorated rapidly until it seemed a black cloud hung over the affair.

Archie, silent and morose, only picked at his food. He paid hardly any attention to his lovely companion, looking up only to stare morosely out the window now and then.

Across the table from him, doing her best to brighten up things a bit, Betty Lou Pemberton felt the bad vibrations that surrounded them. She was even dressed in a civilian dress. The garment was a bit daring for her. It was a low-cut model that showed plenty of her ample cleavage while the tight skirt hugged her hips. Yet it could hardly be compared in sexiness to the slinky outfits worn by Saigon bar girls.

The occasion for the meal was a two-person supper party in Fagin's Saigon apartment. The CIA man, who had arranged a rendezvous of his own with a sexy Red Cross worker named Trixie, was out for the evening. But he had magnanimously allowed his pad to be utilized by the lovers.

The only problem was that there was no romance in the air.

Finally Betty Lou slammed her fork down. "I don't think I can take too much more of this, Archie!"

He looked up at her. "What?"

"You're not paying any attention to me," Betty Lou said.

"Sure I am."

"Then what did I say?" she asked. "You should be able to answer that if your ears have been open."

"You said I wasn't paying any attention to you," Archie replied.

"I mean before that."

Archie thought a moment. "Uh—yeah, I know. You said the meal was good. Right?"

"Wrong! I said I don't think I can take any more of this," Betty Lou said.

Archie straightened up in his chair. "Take any more of what?"

"This!" Betty Lou exclaimed. "*This!* I've never been in such gloomy surroundings since my grandmother died a couple of years ago."

"Okay," Archie said. "What's the matter?"

"You're lousy company, that's *what's* the matter!" she snapped. "You've been walking around for the past two days acting and looking like your best friend had died."

"Maybe so," Archie said. "My best friend— *friends*—are out in hell right now. They might be getting along fine or they might all be dead. And I'm

123

not with them."

"You'd rather be with them than with me, right?" she asked.

"Give me a break, Betty Lou," Archie said. "God! Things are so fucked up right now. I never should've come back here. I was so tore up over you that I couldn't think straight."

"So it's all my fault!" she exclaimed.

"Huh?"

"You just said so!" Betty Lou argued. "I heard you with my own ears."

"All I said was that I was upset about you and didn't have my brain in straight," Archie said defensively. "That wasn't nothing personal against you for Chrissake!"

"In other words," she said slowly in an icy voice, "if I hadn't written you that letter, you wouldn't have come back to Long Binh. Instead, you would have been out there in the jungle with your stupid buddies!"

"Yeah!" Archie yelled. "That's exactly right! And I wish like hell I was out there with them stupid bastards right now! They need me, Betty Lou! Do you understand?" His voice calmed and he spoke with more control but there was still plenty of emotion in his voice. "They *need* me. They're stumbling through the boonies out there trying to find the mission target, and I should be there to help them out. But I'm sitting here in Fagin's apartment safe and sound."

Betty Lou was silent for several long moments before she spoke. "We shouldn't be fighting like this. It just points out how difficult our relationship is."

"I know," Archie said. "It's tough for a woman to be married to a guy like me. Ol' Top Gordon's wife left him because he was too much of a soldier. I guess he spent a hell of a lot of his time with his unit. Even when he was off duty, Top prob'ly thought about his job in the service all the time. That kind of a situation never meant much to me until now."

"I can certainly understand how his wife must have felt. A woman doesn't like her marriage to come in second to anything," Betty Lou said. "Maybe that will change someday, but not in my generation."

"I can understand that too," Archie said. "But the Black Eagles were the first success of my life. When I ain't with the detachment I'm a fuckup — a stockade bird. And that's all I was before I joined up with them. As a matter o' fact, Falconi hisself came and pulled me outta some Saigon dope joint and straightened me up."

"He must have thought you were worth something," Betty Lou said.

"I'm the best tracker, point man, and scout in the United States Army," Archie said. "And that ain't no shit."

"I know," Betty Lou said. "Top Gordon told me about that while he was a patient on my ward last month. You're a unique fellow. And I hate to admit it, but you're a valuable member of that Black Eagle team."

"Not no more," Archie said. "I let 'em down. If there was ever a mission when a good scout and tracker was needed, this one now is it."

"It wasn't your fault, Archie," Betty Lou said. "There was no way you could know that they would be going off to the war. It was just a matter of bad luck."

"—and worse timing," Archie said. "We're always being hit with missions when they're least expected."

"Maybe if they can't find what they're looking for, Falconi will give it up and come back," Betty Lou suggested.

Archie shook his head. "No way. Falconi will keep 'em out there till the job is done or ever'body's dead."

The tears came suddenly in Betty Lou's eyes. "Then I'm glad you're not with them!" she cried.

"Let's not talk about it no more," Archie said. He looked down at his plate. "It'd be a shame to let this good chow go to waste."

"You know something, Archie? You haven't made love to me since you found out you'd missed the mission."

Archie stopped any pretense at trying to eat. "I'm all fucked up, Betty. All—fucked—up."

Betty Lou, who had worked as a psychiatric nurse, now fully understood Archie's torment. She sat silently across the table from him, her hands folded in her lap. After a few moments she picked up her fork again. "You're right, Archie. Let's not waste this good food."

"Mmmm," he mumbled, and the somber meal continued.

The cart, rumbling on its two large wooden wheels, lumbered across the garrison yard. The water buffalo huffed more in irritation than fatigue as it pulled the burden under the guidance of the peasant farmer who clicked directions at the animal in a fashion that had been used for a thousand years in that part of the world. It was as if the man and the beast were as timeless as the primitive environment they inhabited.

Capt. Truong, commander of the guard company, didn't give a damn about the philosophical side of the view. He absentmindedly watched the conveyance from the window of his thatch-roofed headquarters, turned back inside, and looked at Sgt. Dinh sitting patiently in the chair on the other side of the desk.

"Regiment's orders were most emphatic, Comrade Sergeant."

"Regiment's orders generally are," Sgt. Dinh said.

"There are no regular combat troops to spare here at the time," Truong said, ignoring the thinly veiled sarcasm. "Since there is a lack of evidence showing a serious uprising or an in-depth infiltration by enemy personnel, our guard company has been detailed to make a thorough and painstaking reconnaissance of the area around the farms."

Sgt. Dinh rubbed his bad leg. "Our men are soft," he said. "They've spent the previous year doing absolutely nothing but pulling guard on a village of peasants. The only walking they've done has been on roads or well-worn trails through the jungle."

Truong scowled. "Are you saying our unit cannot perform the job?"

Dinh tapped the sergeant insignia on his collar. "Comrade Captain, I will personally guarantee the soldiers will accomplish whatever task is assigned them. The Americans only shot up one of my legs. The other is still good for kicking some lazy *binh-nhi* in the arse!"

"Of course, Comrade Sergeant," Truong said hastily. "Your military record speaks for itself. Also, I am most grateful for the way you have maintained discipline and order in the company ranks. I realize how difficult it must have been under the circumstances of this miserable assignment."

"There are no miserable assignments, Comrade Captain," Dinh said haughtily. "Only miserable soldiers."

"Of course, Comrade Sergeant," Truong said, properly chastised.

Dinh stood up. "With your permission, Comrade Captain, I will assemble the company and exercise my duties as senior non-commissioned officer."

"*Cam on ong,* Comrade Sergeant."

Dinh limped out of the headquarters building. He looked around the well-policed company area. There were no soldiers lolling about or loitering. Everyone in the unit was engaged in some sort of activity—even if not particularly meaningful—so that the general environment of the place was proper and military. This was all Dinh's doing. He resented the fact that the soldiers of the guard company were in safe, easy circumstances while men sent farther south fought and died in ill-supplied misery.

The sergeant smiled to himself. Some of the babies in this outfit were about to grow up—fast!

He pulled his whistle from his shirt pocket and blew into it hard. The shrill, rattling sound echoed over the little garrison and into the distant mountains.

Immediately all men in the area rushed from their

128

work stations and formed up sharply in platoon formations. The only soldiers not answering the call were those on guard duty. Dinh waited a few moments until all the men stood solemn and silent in the position of attention. Then he marched as best he could on his stiff leg to the center of the company square.

"Comrades!" he shouted. "I have called this formation to give you great news. Now, like your embattled brethren in the South, you will have the honor of facing the people's enemies and destroying them!"

The reaction from the soldiers was one of silent confusion. They stood mute, waiting to be further enlightened by their senior sergeant.

"As you all know, we have lost several comrades in the jungle," Dinh continued. "This is something that has shocked many of you because such things are not expected to happen this far north in our country." He paused, then raised his voice high when he spoke again. "But now we know who the interlopers are!"

The platoon ranks wavered a bit as the men looked back and forth at each other, then turned their eyes back to the front.

Dinh wasn't interested in the truth. All he wanted to do was fire up a bunch of badly motivated rear-echelon softies. "A group of gangsters from South Vietnam has invaded our area and is now systematically murdering our soldiers and our peasants. Several bodies of dead men and women were found only two days ago on a commune east of here. The men had been executed with their hands tied behind their backs, and the women violated before their throats were cut!"

There was an angry murmur among the inexperienced young soldiers. It would not have occurred to any of them that what the sergeant said was a bald-faced lie.

"Higher headquarters wanted to send in a regular infantry unit to put things right, but our Comrade Captain Truong would have none of that," Dinh said. "He rightfully insisted these crimes were insults to our guard company, and that it was not only our duty to avenge these deaths, but our right!"

The young men raised in a Communist society had not heard much talk of "rights" before, but they understood the concept just the same.

"So we are going to suspend our regular guard duties and send combat patrols out to hunt down the gangsters and bring them to the people's justice."

A weak cheer erupted, then picked up momentum as the men's enthusiasm built up.

Dinh smiled to himself. He really didn't know who was out there doing all the deadly mischief, but there would soon be a hundred exuberant young soldiers eager for battle to hunt them down and destroy every one of the gangsters.

Dinh took another deep breath, then launched into a fiery speech he had used as a unit leader to the South when the flagging Viet Cong needed rallying after being mauled by the Americans. This time his audience, being well-fed, rested, and healthy, would respond even better. Whoever was roaming those woods would soon face more than they had bargained for.

Falconi lit a cigarette as the Top Gordon finished his vocal report on yet another reconnaissance mission that had been a waste of time.

The sergeant major shook his head slowly in disgust. "We're missing something, sir. I don't know what it is, but whatever will lead us to that damned commo station is just not apparent to us."

Ray Swift Elk, sitting to Top's right, sucked on a blade of grass as he would have done if seated on the South Dakota prairie instead of a jungle clearing in North Vietnam. "These little probes are getting us nowhere," he said. "We haven't had any casualties yet, but pretty soon our luck is going to run out."

"That's right," Calvin Culpepper agreed. "We can't keep running into them NVA without eventually getting hell knocked out of us."

"Or they'll find us," Andrea Thuy said. Her voice remained calm despite the potential disaster she discussed. "And when that happens, there'll be no survivors — only the dead and captured."

"Are you sure you can't remember any logical place the North Vietnamese or Russians might install a hidden complex?" Falconi asked her.

Andrea shook her head. "Sorry. I remember this territory as a child, but there have been a few changes. I've given the matter a lot of thought, but I've come up with nothing."

"Andrea has been a great help in supplementing these old maps," Swift Elk said. "But who knows what the Reds have done to this area? Hell, there's been new construction, alterations on buildings, and even new rice paddies have been dug."

"Okay," Falconi said. "I can see what you're all

driving at. It looks like we're going to have to make one hell of a big effort and go all out on this. I'll have Hank Valverde prepare a resupply list and we'll load up for bear."

Swift Elk spat the grass from between his lips. "Then we'll go hunting. Right, sir?"

"Right," Falconi confirmed. "It'll be a hell of a chance to take."

"I'll say!" Top exclaimed. "We either win in one swoop or end up like Andrea said."

"Remember my old saying," Falconi advised them. "Nobody said this job was going to be easy."

"Yeah!" Calvin Culpepper enjoined. "But nobody said it was gonna be impossible either!"

Chapter Twelve

The ice clinked into the glass. Chuck Fagin turned from his office liquor bar and looked over at Archie Dobbs sitting in the leather chair on the other side of the room. "Sure you don't want me to fix you one?"

"I don't want nothing," Archie said.

"It's no trouble, really," Fagin said.

"Nope."

"Irish whiskey," Fagin said. "You can't beat that."

"Uh uh," Archie insisted.

"Then how about a beer?"

"I don't want nothing, goddamnit!" Archie yelled. "Are you deaf or something, you dumb-ass Fagin you!"

"Hey," Fagin said angrily. "You calm down, buster. This is my office and nobody yells at me here unless he outranks me." He leered at Archie. "And pretty soon you ain't gonna outrank anybody in the entire U.S. Army."

Archie sunk back into his somber mood. "Top is flat gonna kill me, Fagin."

Fagin walked back to his desk and sat down. "Top's personal role in this thing is easy. He's gonna know what he wants to do with you. As for me—I don't know whether to send you back to Nui Dep or just hole you up here at Peterson Field while you wait for your just punishment."

Archie performed an exaggerated shrug. "Fagin. I don't give a shit, awright? Do what you want. I don't care."

"I wish I could have you shot," Fagin joked.

"I wish you could too," Archie said truthfully.

Fagin took a sip of his drink. "How're you and Betty Lou getting along?"

"Not too good," Archie said. "That dinner last night was a total disaster, believe me. We got into a big argument, but made up in the end. Things still ain't good, though."

"I had some problems of my own with the Red Cross broad. She started talking marriage," Fagin said. "Women are trouble."

"Amen to that, brother," Archie agreed. "Betty Lou was right when she said I blamed her for this predicament I'm in. If she hadn't written me that 'Dear John,' I wouldn't have come back to Saigon except on pass."

"If it wasn't for that young woman you'd be out there humping those North Vietnam hills with your pals," Fagin said. "You should've stuck with the whores, Archie. A quick ten bucks and you're happy, while the broad is outta your life."

"I can't help it," Archie said. "Betty Lou got to a side o' me I didn't even know existed. She ripped me up and down, man."

"No good to talk about it," Fagin said taking another drink.

"That's right," Archie said.

The two sat in silence while Fagin absentmindedly consumed his Irish whiskey and soda. After a quarter of an hour, the quiet was broken by the buzzer on Fagin's door. He reached under the desk and pressed the button there making the portal pop open.

A lanky young communications clerk stepped in. He was dressed in a set of semi-starched fatigues that bore the insignia of a specialist fourth grade. "Hi ya, Mister Fagin," he said. He nodded over at Archie. "Hello, Lieutenant."

"Aw, fuck you!" Archie snarled.

"Don't pay no attention to the 'lieutenant,' " Fagin said. "He's grumpy today. What can I do for you?"

"A message come in from the field and the sarge said you was supposed to get a copy of it," the clerk said after displaying a frown at Archie. "It's from them Black Eagles."

Archie leaped to his feet and rushed over. He grabbed the paper from the kid's hands. "Hey, Fagin! They're requesting a resupply drop!"

"Hey, sir!" the clerk said to the bogus officer. "That's for Mister Fagin. You ain't got a need-to-know, y'know?"

"How'd you like to leave here with your ass up between your ears?" Archie asked in a growl.

"Not very much, thank you," the clerk, quite offended, said. "I think I'll just get out of here until proper respect toward enlisted personnel is shown by unnamed persons in this office." He turned and made a dignified escape.

"Lemme go on this, huh, Fagin?" Archie begged.

"What the hell for?" Fagin asked.

"I could make sure the supply drop came off okay," Archie said. "Them aircraft crews don't give a shit sometimes. Especially if they're Vietnamese."

"I'll think about it," Fagin said. He took the message from Archie and read it. "They're asking for some extra ammo and rations mostly. Sounds like they're starting a big push."

"You bet your ass they are!" Archie exclaimed.

"Maybe they already found the target, Archie," Fagin said with a wicked grin. "Maybe they don't need you."

"That's fine," Archie said agreeably. "But, listen, Fagin. You gotta let me go along on the drop."

"Naw. I don't think so, Archie," Fagin said.

"Don't be so chicken-shit, man! Archie protested. "I really want to ride along on the resupply drop. It'd do my heart good to at least kick the stuff they need out the door."

"Speaking of hearts," Fagin said, "mine pumps piss for you."

"That's your way of saying no, ain't it?"

"God! You're smart!"

"Now look, Fagin! You want me to beg? Then I'll beg," Archie said. "Please, please, please, Fagin! Lemme go along on that equipment drop. Please! *Please! PLEASE!*"

"Jesus! Okay," Fagin said. "I guess the aerial delivery boys can always use an extra hand." He paused and looked at Archie's miserable countenance. "And you can help pack the bundles too, I guess."

"Thanks a lot, Fagin," Archie said, grinning

widely. "I owe you, man! I really do."

"I suppose I should feel good about doing a kindness to a fellow human being," Fagin said. "But something tells me you're going to fuck things up again, Archie."

"Who me?"

Fagin sighed and finished the drink. "C'mon, asshole. We get to get things rolling over at the equipment shed. Falconi says they need this stuff quick."

The jungle heat was like a steamy, invisible blanket thrown over the scene. Calvin Culpepper squatted on his haunches and wiped at the heavy rivulets of sweat that ran down his face. He'd been perspiring so heavily the past few hours that the camouflage paint he'd streaked on his features was almost washed away.

The other members of the Calvin's Crapshooters, Hank Valverde and Dean Fotopoulus, had concealed themselves in the nearby brush. The fourth man, Doc Robichaux, had left them to scout ahead.

This particular patrol was the last one before the "big push" that Falconi wanted to launch. It was hoped that Calvin and his men might have some wild good luck and stumble across the communications station.

So far all they'd accomplished was to tramp around the hot-as-hell jungle for three hours.

The brush rustled ahead, and the three Black Eagles tensed for trouble. But it was Doc who emerged from the thick, green cover. He crawled over to Calvin and sat down. "Nothing, man. There ain't a thing out there except more jungle."

"What's the terrain like?" Calvin asked.

"More of this shit," Doc answered pointing around. "But there's a swamp about fifty meters off to the north. It was so overgrown and tangly that I thought I was back home in Louisiana." He uttered a short laugh. "Hell, I started looking out for 'gators and cottonmouths, man."

"I'd hoped we'd find the place," Calvin said mournfully. "That resupply drop is tomorrow. Then we're really going after it."

"I don't like the do-or-die aspect of this thing," Doc said. "But I guess it can't be helped."

"We've always accomplished our missions," Calvin said. "I guess we're too dumb to know when we're licked."

"Either that or we're too dumb to know enough to quit," Doc added.

Calvin checked the time. "Well, we ain't gonna accomplish nothing sitting here. There's another hour or two of patrolling left." He looked closely at Doc. "Are you tired? I can get Dean to spell you on point if you want."

"I ain't tired," Doc said.

"Bullshit," Calvin said. He snapped his fingers in the direction of the Greek-American.

Dean Fotopoulus looked around. "Yeah?"

"Take the point," Calvin said.

"Hup, Sarge," Dean answered. "Which direction?"

"West, then southeast back to the base camp," Calvin said, issuing his informal patrol orders. "Try to keep it around an hour and a half. That's about all the energy or water we got left for."

Dean nodded. He stood up and walked off on the indicated azimuth. Hank followed, Calvin went after him, while Doc Robichaux now brought up the rear.

The small, but determined group of men moved slowly and alertly through the hot, wet environment. They stopped at irregular intervals to listen intently for something — anything — that would give evidence of other human activity in their immediate vicinity.

However, there was nothing but the muted sounds of the jungle.

Dean did his best. His job on the point was extremely difficult because of the need to be security conscious, check for tracks and other signs, and make sure they didn't walk into an ambush.

But that's exactly what they did.

Unknown to the Black Eagles, because of their poor maps, they were close to a farming village. This particular establishment was deep in the monsoon forest because the inhabitants were actually political prisoners rather than regular peasants. They had been sentenced to hard labor, and their program of punishment was filled with hardships and harsh treatment. The North Vietnamese Government liked to keep such places out of sight. Therefore, the guard positions around the place were established as much to keep people *out* as to keep them *in*.

The first AK47 rounds were fired by an ill-trained, inexperienced North Vietnamese trooper who emptied an entire magazine of thirty rounds over the heads of Calvin's Crapshooters.

Dean responded with three shots from his M16. The first punched the NVA in the chest causing him to flop over on his back. The guy sat up more out of instinct than desire, and caught a second slug in the forehead that made his pith helmet spin crazily off his head.

The third round from Dean's muzzle slapped harmlessly into a tree. The target for this particular bullet had been a veteran trooper with plenty of fighting experience in the South. He'd hit the ground hard and fast when the first fusillade kicked off. The NVA's further response had been to shoot back — and to do so as fast as possible.

The 7.62-millimeter rounds buzzed angrily around Dean's head, and he too made use of Mother Earth. Hank Valverde had come up behind him and moved to the right. He quickly covered his buddy with sweeping volleys of full-automatic fire.

A yell indicated the NVA had been hit. The following silence confirmed it.

Calvin had also moved forward and the situation made him exceedingly edgy. "Pull back, dudes," he ordered tersely. "Let's go."

His uneasiness was well-founded because in less than sixty seconds a detachment of enemy soldiers could be heard rushing toward them.

In the meantime Doc Robichaux had moved up on line so that three M16s faced the incoming attack. Each weapon, with the exception of Hank's, fired rapidly on semi-auto. Hank Valverde, as the fire team's automatic rifleman, had his selector properly set for that deadly duty. He pumped out rhythmic fire bursts of five and six rounds to the front.

Doc, on the left, sensed movement to one side of the action. He glanced that way in time to catch sight of two NVAs trying to pull a flanking movement.

The Cajun swung his weapon in that direction and fired quickly. One enemy trooper spun around crazily before collapsing out of sight in the brush. But his buddy kept coming.

"Enemy left!" Doc shouted. He fired again, this time shooting no less than four rounds.

The incoming Red trooper suddenly looked like he'd bumped into an invisible wall. He fell back on his ass, then flopped over on one side and died.

Hank had a similar experience on the right, but his full-automatic fire, while a bit inaccurate, discouraged the NVA on that side enough to hesitate.

"Let's leave this unhappy place," Calvin said. "In a hurry!"

The team backpedaled while still throwing lead out to the front. When they'd finally broken contact, they turned and continued their retreat.

A half hour later Calvin felt it was safe enough to give the guys a break. He called a halt and settled down as their perimeter was automatically formed.

Dean Fotopoulus, his eyes peering outward, spoke to his buddies around him. "Well, this was the last patrol before Falconi's big push. Looks like we didn't pull it off either."

"That means do-or-die," Doc said.

"Damn you, Doc!" Calvin swore. "I hate your choice of words, you know that?"

"I ain't really crazy about 'em either, Calvin," Doc said. Then he repeated the phrase to himself.

Do or Die!

Chapter Thirteen

The C-119 "Flying Boxcar" belonged to the South Vietnamese Air Force, and it was in such need of a good overhaul. The old plane, which sported loosened rivets, rust, and leaky hydraulic lines, had seen service over fifteen years earlier during the 187th Airborne Regimental Combat Team's combat parachute jump in the Korean War.

Archie Dobbs, strapped into a secondhand, well-worn B12 parachute, grimaced with each miss of the aircraft's dual Pratt and Whitney engines. These motors were so erratic that the pilot had to fight a constant battle to keep the big plane on level flight. The Oriental airman struggled with flaps, throttle, and elevator trim while his airship pitched and yawed. There was so much violence in these movements that Archie felt as if his teeth were being rattled in his head.

The interior was as worn and tacky as the exterior, with missing seat braces and even a couple of glassless portholes. Wind whipped through these openings and blue the torn canvas seat racks against the bulkheads.

Normally, equipment bundles would have been dropped from the aircraft with the monorail assembly that was mounted in the overhead. Unfortunately, the device had long been inoperative because of poor maintenance and a lack of proper parts. Therefore, since the rear "clamshell" that held the two exit doors was gone anyway and there was a wide opening in the rear of the cargo fuselage, it was necessary to kick the Black Eagles' supplies out the back. This meant physically wrestling the heavy loads by hand. For that reason, the Vietnamese crew had been very happy to have Archie's company for the delivery.

The Vietnamese crew chief, a wiry little sergeant, came out of the pilot's compartment and stepped down on the deck of the fuselage. He brought Archie half a canteen cup of green tea. The rough flight would not permit a fuller container without a lot of spilling. The sergeant handed the brew to the American without a word.

Archie took the cup and gratefully drank the lukewarm stuff, savoring the flavor and the pickup he knew he would get from the caffeine.

The sergeant leaned down and shouted in Archie's ear over the deafening, erratic roar of the engines. "Pretty soon we reach DZ, GI."

"Yeah," Archie yelled back. "If this bird can make it."

The AFRVN man laughed. "Oh, we make it. Don't worry. Good airplane. I take care of it myself."

"Sure, guy. I'll bet you're a whiz with spit and

143

barbed wire," Archie growled to himself. He involuntarily shuddered when the left engine's RPM suddenly leaped forward making the big plane yaw crazily and slide through the sky. He spilled the tea all over his lap. "Goddamnit!"

The wild, uncontrolled maneuver caused the sergeant to fall on the floor as the aircraft shuddered and shook violently. But it quickly settled down. The Vietnamese laughed. "You see? Good airplane. No crash, eh?"

"Maybe not this time," Archie hollered at the outrageously optimistic Oriental. He handed back the empty cup. "This was a useless fucking idea."

The sergeant got to his feet and took the utensil. "You take nap. I wake you for the drop. I need help to push out bundle. You take one, I take one. Okay, GI?"

"Okay." Archie watched the Vietnamese go back up to pilot country. Normally the Black Eagle could take a catnap on a running roller coaster, but there was something decidedly more dangerous about this unkempt flying coffin than an amusement park ride. It all added up to Archie being nervous enough to stay wide awake.

He stayed that way for the next three quarters of an hour until the sergeant came back. "Pretty quick now. Come on."

"I'm ready," Archie yelled back. He was anxious to make sure that the Black Eagles received the supplies they obviously needed so badly.

The two bundles that were to be dropped were properly rigged and set in the middle of the cargo deck. Archie quickly attached the static line of one to

144

the anchor cable that ran the length of the fuselage. The AFRVN sergeant took care of the other. Then the two of them wrestled the heavy packs to the edge of the door and poised them to be tumbled out into the sky.

Archie looked out at the tail boom to check for the red and green lights. But the Vietnamese guy tapped him on the shoulder and shook his head. "No light."

"What?" Archie bellowed back. "They don't work either?"

"Don't worry. Co-pilot wave to us when it time for drop," the Vietnamese yelled.

Archie spat out into the clear air. "That figures," he muttered under his breath.

The aircraft continued in its pitching, yawing line of flight. Archie stared down over the dark green of the North Vietnamese jungle. They were flying so low that the propeller blast was blowing the tops of trees violently back and forth. He estimated their altitude at between two and three hundred feet above this canopy of vegetation.

Archie's conscience had gone into overtime in punishing him. His mind kept telling him that his buddies were down there facing death while trying to pull off a near-impossible mission. Archie had failed them because of his lack of emotional control. They were on an operation and he was in a big, lumbering airplane with a half-assed South Vietnamese Air Force NCO who probably thought the C-119 would keep flying as long as its *karma* meant for it to do so.

"Look! Look!" the sergeant shouted.

Archie turned and saw the co-pilot standing in the doorway leading to the large cockpit. The officer, who was keeping a close eye on his watch, looked up to grin and give a "thumbs-up" sign. Archie grinned back without much enthusiasm.

"Hey! Get ready!" the sergeant hollered.

Archie nodded. He kept his eyes plastered on the co-pilot. Finally the guy looked up from his watch and signaled frantically.

The South Vietnamese NCO pushed his bundle to the edge of the door and tipped it out. Archie did the same and watched the big canvas-covered package clear the aircraft.

Then he jumped after it.

Not a sound could be discerned from the small garrison square despite that fact that a hundred men occupied the area. These soldiers belonged to the guard company commanded by Capt. Truong, who was assisted by the veteran Sgt. Dinh.

The reason they were drawn up so smartly in front of their thatched billets was the impending visit of their regimental commander. This man, a scarred campaigner named Drung, had sent word of this occasion by dispatch. The messenger was a senior lieutenant who stayed long enough to add encouragement to Truong and Dinh in their efforts to make sure their troops were squared away and standing tall. He accomplished this by threatening them with accusations of incompetence, ineptitude, and acts of reactionism.

It scared the hell out of Truong. He bellowed and threatened the men he thought were not making things neat and orderly in the little military post.

Sergeant Dinh, on the other hand, was an old soldier and had less education. The NCO was a firm believer in the physical approach to getting one's points across. He kicked and pummeled the slow and lazy in a frenzy that was effective despite his bad leg.

The end result of this twenty-four hours of local terrorism was a company turned out sharp and smart, ready and waiting for their regimental commander.

It is an unwritten law in all armies that the lower-ranking people have to toe the line and be prompt. For colonels and above, the opposite is true. Col. Drung stayed faithful to this tradition by showing up two hours late.

Since Truong and Dinh had fallen the men out two hours ahead of the scheduled time of arrival, the soldiers had been standing in the hot tropical sun for a bit more than four hours waiting for the regimental commander's appearance. Several had fainted, others vomited from dizziness, and all licked their dry lips as bodies, parched from heavy perspiration, began to rapidly dehydrate.

The colonel arrived in a Soviet UAZ-69A command car. He waited while the driver jumped from the vehicle and scurried around to open the door for him. Then he stepped from the vehicle and took Truong's salute.

"*Chao ong,* Comrade Colonel," the young captain said with a snappy salute.

"*Chao ong,*" the colonel said impatiently.

"The guard company is prepared for inspection," Truong announced nervously.

"Then let's get it over with, Comrade Captain,"

147

Col. Drung said. He marched rapidly to the first platoon and took Sgt. Dinh's salute. Here he stopped and displayed a fond smile. "Hello, old comrade."

"*Chao ong,* Comrade Colonel," Dinh said. He and the officer had served together for more than a year during the fight with the French. A bit later they were together again, but that time in the South against the Americans. Dinh's nasty wound had taken him out of active combat.

"How is your leg, Comrade Sergeant?" Drung asked.

"Only a bit stiff, Comrade Colonel," Dinh answered properly.

"But your courage is unbent, true?"

"Yes, Comrade Colonel," Dinh answered. "I am always ready to sacrifice what is necessary for the advancement of Marxism."

"Good soldier, Comrade!" the colonel said. He lowered his voice and whispered. "Now let's inspect this miserable company and get down to serious business, eh?"

"Yes, Comrade Colonel!"

The senior officer's wishes were attended to and the company was dismissed back to duty after a rapid ten-minute look-over. Then, signaling them to follow, Colonel Drung led Truong and Dinh to the headquarters building.

The colonel took Truong's chair behind the desk. "A most serious situation has arisen in this sector."

Truong and Dinh stood in silence, waiting to be fully briefed.

Drung lit a cigarette. "There is a communications station here. I'm sure you know of the big complex to

148

the southeast, true?"

"Yes, Comrade Colonel," Truong answered. "I recall when it was constructed a bit more than a year ago."

"But we are not allowed in the vicinity," Dinh added. "We did not know it was for communications."

"It most certainly is," Drung said. "And we fear the Western imperialists have discovered its existence—but not its location."

Although Truong couldn't perceive the big picture, Dinh most certainly did. "Then the attacks we have reported are not from escaping peasants or ragged partisans, Comrade Colonel?"

"Most certainly not," Drung answered. "We fear that a highly organized and trained team of specialists has invaded the area for the express purpose of finding and destroying the complex. It would be a great blow to our cause if they succeeded. And it will help your men's morale and fighting spirit if they knew whom they faced."

Dinh smiled. "Excuse me, Comrade Colonel, but I have already given them such a story as a way of stoking their fires of enthusiasm."

The colonel laughed. "You still follow the policy we used with the comrades in the Viet Cong, eh? Very well. Your propaganda has turned out to be true."

Truong was excited. "Do you want us to find them, Comrade Colonel?"

"Yes," Drung answered. "We have no regular troops available. The pressure on our Viet Cong comrades in the South has caused a great drain of

149

manpower. Therefore we must rely on this guard company to ferret out and destroy the infiltrators."

"Excuse me, Comrade Colonel," Sergeant Dinh said. "But it is time for realism in a situation like this. Most of our men are inexperienced youngsters. The only veterans we have are men like myself who are unable to perform arduous field duties because of physical disabilities."

"Yes, old comrade, but, as you say, all the NCOs are seasoned veterans. You sergeants and corporals can teach them much." He studied Dinh's features. "You show no enthusiasm, Comrade Sergeant. But suppose I assured you there would be no shortage of what you will need."

"We need helicopter support," Dinh said bluntly. "Both for gunships and transportation."

"You shall have it," Drung said.

Truong finally found his tongue. "That would make my hundred men be like five hundred, Comrade Colonel."

"Of course," Drung agreed.

"The invaders could not number more than two dozen or so," Dinh said in professional judgment.

"Five hundred against twenty-four," Drung said. "I think this battle is won." Then he added, "But I don't think there are that many of them."

"One dozen, two dozen, or three dozen," Dinh said. "They are as good as dead."

"Yes," Drung said. He looked at Truong. "Even a guard company commanded by an inexperienced commander could not lose with unlimited supplies and aerial support." He nodded toward Dinh. "And, of course, you have seasoned non-commissioned officers, Comrade Captain. I strongly advise you to take advantage of their experience and counsel."

"Yes, Comrade Colonel!" Truong exclaimed.

"When do we start, Comrade Colonel?" Dinh asked.

Drung stood up and set his pith helmet on his head. Now!"

"Now?" Truong questioned him.

"Even as we speak, the helicopters are on their way here," Drung said.

"The victory is assured," Dinh said confidently. "The only question is when."

Chapter Fourteen

Archie Dobbs, upside down and falling at an angle, caught a quick glimpse of the C-119 between his legs as it flew away from him. He could also see, for an even briefer instant, the startled face of the surprised Vietnamese Air Force sergeant with eyes and mouth wide open in unabashed shock.

Another thing that caught Archie's attention was how terrifyingly close the tops of the trees were. It seemed he could reach out and touch them. He frantically yanked on the ripcord of the ancient parachute he wore.

The spring-loaded pilot chute in the backpack leaped out and caught the wind, dragging the rest of the canopy behind it as the jumper plunged ground-ward. The nylon seemed to move in slow motion as it deployed, then suddenly the expanse of parachute cracked loudly as it opened violently.

Archie's wild fall came to an abrupt halt and he swung out, then slammed into the ground flat on his back. "Oh, shit!" he exclaimed involuntarily. He rolled over on his stomach and struggled to his hands and knees. The sound of approaching footsteps alarmed him, but he was still a bit stunned from the jump to react quickly. When he finally came to a fuller awareness of his surroundings he could see a pair of tiger-stripe camouflaged trousers bloused over a pair of canvas-and-leather jungle boots in front of his face.

Archie looked up into the face of the man glaring down at him.

"You're late, Dobbs!" Top Gordon snapped. "Get on your feet and give us a hand getting these bundles off the drop zone."

"Yes—yes, Sergeant Major," Archie said. He struggled to his feet and began freeing himself from the parachute.

Top looked over the jump equipment with a disapproving gaze. "You're lucky that rig worked, Dobbs. I saw the canopy deploy and it blew out three panels when it opened. The whole damned thing's all wore out and probably years overdue for a rigger check."

"The gods favor the righteous, Top," Archie said, now fully recovered from the quick ordeal.

Malpractice McCorckel, ever the "mama medic," trotted up with a concerned expression on his face. "Jesus, Archie! That was a crazy stunt if I ever saw one. You slammed into the ground on your back, man! How're you feeling?" He grabbed Archie's head and quickly examined his eyes, nose, and ears for the telltale bleeding of a skull fracture or violent concussion.

"Hell, I'm okay," Archie said.

"Yeah," Malpractice said. "I guess you are." Then he looked down at the front of Archie's trousers. "Did you piss in your pants, asshole?"

"Hell, no!" Archie protested. "I spilled tea on myself. You wanta smell?"

"I ain't putting my face down to your crotch," Malpractice said.

Blue Richards and Salty O'Rourke had secured the bundles and dragged them off the drop zone into the protective cover of the jungle. Now they joined the others. Blue, grinning widely, came up and pounded Archie on the back. "Hey, you ol' Archie, I knowed you couldn't stay away from us."

Top Gordon growled, "But he's gonna wish like hell he did before I'm finished with him."

"Hi ya, Archie," Salty said offering his hand. "Did you get that 'Jody' who took your gal?"

"Hell, she's still my gal," Archie said. "But that's a long story. Let's get the hell outta here. All my gear is packed away in one o' them bundles."

Archie and Top's Terrors quickly left the site and gathered around the recently delivered supplies. Carrying poles had already been cut and prepared for the burdens. Blue and Salty took one while Archie and Malpractice shouldered the other. Top led the way back to the base camp.

It took the fire team two hours to travel up the tortuous hill to the safety of the Black Eagle base camp. Because of the energy-sapping heat, they were forced to take frequent breaks. All the good food and beer that Archie had consumed in Saigon was sweated out in the first fifteen minutes. Since he had no canteen he had to rely on the willing but limited charity of the others as they shared their water with him.

Archie, despite being new to the area, took advan-

154

tage of his natural skills to orient himself with his surroundings during the trek. He felt right at home by the time they reached camp. A hoarse whisper, sounding the challenge, came out of the brush.

"*Calcitra—*"

"*Clunis*," Top properly replied using the counter-sign.

"C'mon in, guys," said Paulo Garcia. Ray's Rough-necks were on guard duty at that particular time. The Portuguese-American nodded a friendly, surprised greeting when he spotted Archie. "Hey, AWOL, glad to see you!"

"Glad to see you too, Paulo," Archie said. "I hear you guys are wandering around here lost."

"That's the truth," Paulo admitted.

"Shaddup!" Top snapped. He motioned to the team. "Keep moving and knock off the bullshit!"

Archie struggled with the others through the natural camouflage surrounding the camp and stepped out into the interior. The place was cleared away under the protective, heavy covering of thick inter-twined tree limbs overhead. Individual hootches made of palms laid over frameworks of thin branches were scattered around the area. Each member of the detachment had constructed one for sleeping quarters, and there was a place to store their gear.

The other men had spotted Archie. They were genuinely glad to see him and did nothing to hide their feelings. Those not on duty came up to the scout with wide grins and handshakes.

Calvin Culpepper, his ebony face alight with a smile, hugged the scout. "Man, we've needed you, Archie."

Doc Robichaux and Dean Fotopoulus didn't say much, but the hard claps to the former AWOL's shoulders aptly demonstrated their happiness at seeing him.

"Lemme set this thing down, guys," Archie said. "You're about to beat me to death." After he and Blue set their burden on the ground at Hank Valverde's directions, the scout spotted Falconi sitting outside his own domicile. He looked nervously at the others. "Well, I'd better get this over with."

"You still got me to deal with, don't forget!" Top warned him.

"Right, Sergeant Major."

Archie walked over to his commander and nodded to him with a sheepish expression. "Hi ya, sir. I'm back. Sorry about—"

Falconi, surprised to see the scout, was momentarily caught off guard. He even started to smile, but he caught himself. "You sonofabitch!"

"Yes, sir."

There was a rustle inside the hootch and Andrea Thuy crawled out. She didn't hide her pleasure at seeing an old friend. The young woman leaped to her feet and quickly embraced Archie. "Hey, you old horse thief!"

"Damn! Andrea!" Archie sputtered hugging her back. "I didn't expect to ever see you again. Much less run into you on a mission."

Andrea kissed his cheek. "I hear you have woman trouble, Archie."

Archie grinned. "Hell, no! Not any more. My—"

"Knock it off!" Falconi snapped at the woman. "Don't be nice to that AWOL bastard."

Andrea smiled. "He's not AWOL now, Robert. He's come home."

"Yes, sir," Archie said. He let Andrea go and squatted down beside Falconi. "I hear you guys have been having trouble finding that place you're supposed to blow up," he said with a hint of superiority in his voice.

Falconi reached inside his fatigue jacket and produced one of the old French maps they had been using. He spread it out on the ground. "Study this thing," he said. "That goddamned place is somewhere in the area. We can't find it."

Archie bent over the map. "Where exactly are we on this thing?"

Falconi put his finger on a spot. "We are here."

Archie studied the contour lines and other topographical features for a couple of minutes. Then he too pointed down at the document. "I'd start looking about there."

"Okay," Falconi said. "That's exactly what we'll do. We'll be leaving in two hours."

"Hey!" Archie said. "My gear is still in one o' them bundles."

"Then you'd better get the goddamned stuff outta there, hadn't you?" Falconi growled. "Or you're going to be prowling this jungle as naked as the day you were born."

The guard in front of the officers' mess watched with sleepy interest as the man in the civilian clothes parked the jeep in front of the building. When the driver got out and approached the door, the soldier

157

stopped him with an praised hand. "Need to see your ID, Mister."

"You bet," Chuck Fagin said. He flashed his wallet CIA identification.

"Okay," the young guy said.

Fagin went into the messhall and stopped to glance around at the crowd there. They were doctors and nurses mostly from the various hospitals at Long Binh. When he saw Betty Lou Pemberton waving at him, Fagin smiled a greeting and walked over to join her.

He sat down at the table. "Hi, Betty Lou. How're you doing?"

Betty Lou ignored the salutation. "He's not coming back, is he?"

Fagin shook his head. "Nope. And I really didn't expect him to. The Vietnamese crew said he bailed out right after they kicked the bundles loose."

She frowned and her mouth trembled. "That damned Archie!" she hissed. The young woman was so tense that her fists were clinched tight. But after a moment she relaxed and looked at Fagin. "I guess I didn't expect him back either."

"I knew he'd jump in with the equipment," Fagin said. "He probably planned the whole thing from the moment he heard about the supply drop."

"I suppose I should just hope and pray I'll see him again," Betty Lou said.

"Don't worry," Fagin said. "Those guys are a damned capable bunch." Before he could add any more comments, the Vietnamese waiter appeared. The two ordered their lunch.

Betty Lou spoke again after the man had left them.

158

"How long will Archie be here in Vietnam?"

Fagin shrugged. "If I know him, he'll stick with the detachment as long as it's in existence."

"Hasn't anyone in the Black Eagles ever finished their tour and left?" Betty Lou asked.

Fagin knew that in the history of Falconi's unit the only men who had left the unit had been those killed. He didn't think it prudent or kind to speak of that. "They're all very loyal to their commanding officer."

"You are too," Betty Lou said.

"Naw!" Fagin scoffed. "Not me!"

"And you're loyal to every one of those men too," Betty Lou said. "I'm a trained psychiatric nurse, Chuck. I can see a lot you don't think I do."

"Really?" He leaned forward in interest. "Tell me, Nurse Pemberton. Just what do you see?"

"I see a man who has a belligerent relationship with a group of people for whom he has a great deal of affection," Betty Lou said. "And I can't really figure out why. Unless it's some sort of *machismo* in which men don't want to show any emotional weakness."

"It's all very coldly and logically calculated on my part," Fagin said. "As a matter of fact, I go out of my way to make those wonderful bastards hate my guts."

Betty Lou was genuinely shocked and puzzled. "But why?"

"Because they're up to their ears in shit," Chuck said. "I could spare you a bit, but I won't."

"Go ahead," she urged him.

"Those Black Eagles catch the worst missions under the worst conditions," Fagin explained. "There

159

are factors and situations that screw over them in a terrible way. Even that bunch of fighters are impotant to strike back at mismanagement and apathy from the upper echelons who issue their orders."

"It sounds like they should be frustrated to the point of insanity or rebellion," Betty Lou observed.

"But they do have a method and a place to stage a backlash and vent that pent-up anger and rage," Fagin said with a satisfied grin. "They have me. I take the blame for everything. If supplies are late or short, I let them think it's my fault. If backup or support fails to show, I let them think I failed in my job. That way, there is a real, live tormentor for them to hate and yell at." He grinned ruefully. "I suppose I should be grateful that none of them have tried to kill me yet, huh?"

"Do you really think that much of them?"

"Yes," Fagin said. "It's almost the same situation and reason that you sent a 'Dear John' to Archie despite the fact that you're in love with him."

The waiter appeared with their meal and wordlessly served them. Betty Lou picked up the glass of beer by her plate. "Here's to the Black Eagles—wherever they are."

"Here's to the Black Eagles," Fagin said echoing her words. "Wherever they are and whatever they are doing."

"May God help them," Betty Lou added fervently.

"Sometimes I wonder if that will be enough," Fagin said.

160

Chapter Fifteen

An atmosphere of confidence suddenly appeared with Archie Dobbs's arrival into the operational area.

There was no doubt in anyone's mind about him.

Archie Dobbs was a fuckup.

In garrison, in town, and even when wounded and confined in the hospital, he broke the rules. A lot of these actions were stupid, useless pranks that included loose women and plenty of beer. This, unfortunately, had always been the story of Archie's life. As a kid in Cambridge, Massachusetts, he'd been a chronic truant and juvenile delinquent. His entry into the army had been encouraged by an exasperated social worker who was growing sick and tired of the seventeen-year-old and his constant flaunting of society's norms and expectations.

The military brought out a hidden talent in Archie. Once out of the city and into the wild and unmarked boondocks, the kid had a homing instinct and a talent for orientation that would put a migratory bird to shame. He was a natural tracker and compass man who could move faultlessly from Point "A" to Point "B" on this old planet despite weather, visibility, terrain, or distance.

This ability could be traced back to his ancestors. These folks of merry old England had earned their bread in a particularly adventurous manner. They were poachers. No earl, duke, or lord of a manor, not even the King of England, could keep the persistent Dobbs clan from hunting and fishing his private domains. Generations of following this dangerous trade and marrying into families who followed the same lifestyle had developed genes in which the necessary skills of stealth, tracking, and directional orientation had evolved to the maximum.

To this day in the English county of Nottinghamshire, there is a tale out of the misty past which involves a man named Dobbs who, rather than shrieking in agony while being drawn and quartered, shouted out how he had enjoyed a lord's roasted venison—the very crime for which he was being painfully executed.

No wonder there was a hell of a rebellious nature to Archie's makeup.

Now, with those skills guiding his actions, Sgt. Archie Dobbs led the Black Eagle detachment down the hills from their base camp in search of the skillfully camouflaged and hidden commo center they were charged with destroying.

This was an all-out effort. The entire detachment, not just one fire team, participated. Even the machine-gun team of Gunnar Olson and Tiny Burke plodded along in the middle of the formation. Their heavy-duty M60 with its lethal load of 7.62-millimeter rounds was primed and ready for action. And Tiny carried many other bandoliers of linked ammunition for whenever the gun demanded to be fed.

Archie moved as rapidly as possible, but his speed was actually quite slow. He had to keep in mind that there were sixteen other men behind him. All were loaded with different types of combat gear, and they had to be able to travel quietly through the jungle. Rushing them would not only create havoc with noise discipline, it would also exhaust the men. It was a hell of a lot harder to march within a column than it was to lead it at the front.

Archie threw up his hand to silently signal a halt. Dwayne Simpson behind him stopped and passed the mute command back.

Archie knelt down and studied the ground in front of him. There was something unnatural and alien in its appearance. Although no footprints could be discerned, the lay of the grass and leaves on the earth disturbed the scout. He crawled slowly and deliberately twenty meters down from his original position, then retraced the path. He went ten meters up in the opposite direction, then returned to starting point. He pulled the Prick-Six radio off his shoulder and whispered in it.

A minute later Lt. Col. Robert Falconi, with Andrea Thuy fast on his heels, appeared at his side. "Yeah, Archie?" he asked in a whisper.

"Look at that ground," Archie said in a low voice. "Somebody's been through here and has been sweeping his tracks away."

Andrea could also see the sign after Archie pointed it out. She stepped around Falconi to give the evidence a closer study on her own. "How many some-bodies are we talking about?" she asked.

"A hell of a lot of 'em," Archie said. "I went up that way and—" He pointed in the opposite direction. "—down there. I found some places where they'd been careless. This here's a trail o' sorts, and I'm willing to bet it goes to that commo station."

"It seems a logical conclusion," Falconi said. "Take us on down there. We'll have a look."

"Yes, sir." Archie waited a couple of minutes for Falconi and Andrea to return to their position in the middle of the column. Then he motioned to Dwayne to follow.

The Black Eagles moved down the trail even more slowly now. Archie's cool nerves slowly began to tighten up and he began darting his eyes about apprehensively as his breath quickened. Every inborn thread of self-preservation told him to stop and go back. But the mission was paramount, and that goddamned communications station had to be found and blown away.

Finally Archie did stop. His instincts of danger were making him irritable and aggressive like a cornered animal. He raised his M16 and held the muzzle forward in a gesture of defiance and self-defense.

Then the jungle in front of him exploded with AK47 rounds and the shouts of command in Vietnamese.

"Tien len!"
"Mau len!"
"Di ra!"

Archie returned fire and stumbled backward as the branches around his head were cut by incoming slugs. Dwayne Simpson moved forward to cover him while Jesse Makalue went to the left to lend a hand too.

Within a few short seconds it was obvious that a large unit of NVA had been waiting for them and had now launched an all-out attack in the confining terrain.

Falconi, back in the middle of the column with the Command Element, recalled some higher ground fifty meters to the rear. He shouted orders into his Prick-Six that were picked up by the three fire-team leaders. Then he grabbed Gunnar Olson by his muscular arms.

"When we hit that elevation, I want you and Tiny to set up to give support for three hundred and sixty degrees."

"Yes, sir!" Gunnar the Gunner said. He turned and beckoned to Tiny Burke. "C'mon! And make sure there's two cans ready at all times."

"Okay, Gunnar," Tiny replied in his deep voice. "I'll do real good. Don't you worry none about that."

The two hurried their pace as best they could as the firing to the front built up at an alarming rate. Andrea cranked a round into the chamber of her M16. "I'll cover the machine-gun crew, Robert."

Falconi nodded. "Go for it, Andrea. We've got to keep them in operation."

The actual maneuvering of the detachment was damned good, but Ray's Roughnecks, up at the very front, were having a hell of a time breaking contact from the growing pressure of the attackers.

Archie Dobbs stayed with the fire team as a squad of five Red soldiers, their Kalashnikov assault rifles

165

on full auto, stormed straight at them throwing out angry buzzes of flying steel. The bullets smacked into trees, cut leaves loose to flutter down on Ray and his guys, and sang off into the distance as richochets.

The Roughnecks were well-drilled. Paulo Garcia acted as the automatic rifleman while the others fired rapid, well-spaced volleys in an overlapping pattern.

For a couple of terrifying seconds there seemed to be no effect, but suddenly the middle NVA spun completely around and dropped out of sight into the brush. Two more pitched over onto their faces. The surviving duo managed to get three more steps before they were blown away by Paulo's aggressive salvos of bursts of a half-dozen rounds.

Fresh fire came in over their heads. This was from Top's Terrors and Calvin's Crapshooters, who had gotten themselves into good positions to lend support.

"Okay!" Ray yelled. "Go for it!"

The Roughnecks—and Archie—forgot about shooting back now. They simply turned and ran like hell toward the others. It took only seconds for them to rush up the hill into the quick but effective perimeter of defense that Falconi had organized on the fly.

Gunnar the Gunner now saw his chance to contribute to the effort. His big weapon chugged away at one hundred rounds of sustained fire. "Keep the ammo nice and straight, Tiny!" he yelled over the sound of his own shooting.

"Okay, Gunnar," Tiny said in his deep, slow voice. "I'll do good. Don't you worry none."

The metal links of the ammo belts clinked and

pinged as they bounced away from the weapon. Tiny Burke, his huge body prone beside the machine gun, stayed ready to lend any assistance needed as he allowed the linked belt to slide across his huge paws into the M60's receiver.

Andrea continued to act as their cover, keeping on the alert to make sure no unexpected infiltrators made it into the position to knock out the M60.

The Black Eagles farther forward instinctively ducked their heads as the rounds slapped the air a few inches above them. Salty O'Rourke and Blue Richards, close to each other, spotted a team of NVA coming in from the side. But before they could respond to the threat, Gunnar the Gunner's fusillades shifted and sent the green-uniformed enemy soldiers tumbling to the ground in bloody piles.

Falconi, only a couple of meters away from the machine-gun crew, nodded encouragement to them as he spoke into the Prick-Six. "Team Leaders!" he yelled over the din of the M60. "Get those god-damned grenadiers to work!"

Dwayne Simpson, Salty O'Rourke, and Doc Robichaux were all in separate teams, but when they began pumping 40-millimeter grenades out through their M203s, it was like a well-rehearsed, syncopated operation.

Gunnar's efforts continued to blast into the now-hesitant ranks of NVA. Then the grenades began exploding in the Reds' midst for a full ten minutes of Black Eagle hell. The effect of the fire was so devastatingly evident that Archie Dobbs leaped to his feet and emptied a magazine toward the enemy.

"Calcitra clunis!" he yelled in happy rage.

"Hey!" Swift Elk hollered at him over the din of shooting. "You'd better bet that *clunis* of yours down before Gunnar the Gunner puts a couple of rounds in it."

Archie wisely flopped back to Mother Earth.

The firing eased off enough finally for the Black Eagles to hear the shouted commands of the NVA squad leaders. Within moments, the Reds made another effort. It was an embarrassing moment for Gunnar Olson. He and Tiny were in the middle of a barrel change.

"Damn, Tiny!" the Norwegian-American gunner hissed through clinched teeth. *"Skynd Dem*—hurry up!"

Andrea, alarmed, crawled over to see if she could lend a hand with the operation. If the machine gun weren't brought into action soon, the entire battle could disintegrate into a wild route for the Black Eagles.

Ray's Roughnecks caught the initial charge—as they had when the battle begun—and they became alarmed as the enemy force in front of them rapidly built up. Dwayne Simpson did the best he could with his grenade launcher, but it was not enough. The other grenadiers tried to help out. Unfortunately they couldn't see well enough to properly place their rounds for the maximum killing effect.

The Red soldiers pressed relentlessly forward in growing numerical strength.

But Gunnar the Gunner got back into the act and the situation reversed itself. Some well-placed grazing fire swept deep and wide in front of the Black Eagle position.

Top and Calvin sent their two grenadiers forward to join the Roughnecks. Now the NVA fell in groups of three and four as they were swept with slugs from M16s and the M60 along with spitting, tearing shrapnel from the grenades.

"Lui lai! Lui lai!"

Falconi, understanding the Vietnamese command to retreat, allowed his men another two minutes of interrupted firing. Then he issued his own orders to end the fighting.

"Eagle to all Eagles. Cease fire and prepare to move back."

Archie Dobbs, when he'd gotten the word, rushed back from the front to find the command element. He reported in to see what was on the lieutenant colonel's mind. Falconi wanted to ask a couple of questions.

"Do you think we're close to the objective, Archie?"

"Yes, sir," Archie answered. "I sure as hell do."

"I agree," Falconi said. "But we can't find it now. The local NVA unit is obviously fully alerted now. Any group this size would attract too much attention and would never pinpoint the exact location."

"Right," Archie said taking the hint. "I'll bet I could find it on my lonesome, sir. Once I made a sketch map of the layout, you could figure out the best way to get rid o' the goddamned place."

Andrea had left the machine gun to rejoin Falconi. She winked at Archie. "What chance does a girl have to go along with a good-looking guy like you?"

"Aw, hell, Andrea!" Archie scoffed.

Falconi was not in a humorous mood. "You're not

going with him, Andrea. I can't risk two people on a hairy undertaking like that."

Archie shook his head. "Gee, sir!" he said sardonically. "You don't know how goddamned good it makes me feel to hear you say that."

Chapter Sixteen

The darkness of the night is a friend. If parents taught their children this, there would be no reason for nightlights in nurseries nor childhood fears of "bogeymen" lurking unseen in the unlit corners of the kids' bedrooms.

The philosophy behind this is simple:

What you can't see, can't see you either!

Archie Dobbs followed this reasoning to the letter as he crept through the night down the mountain from the Black Eagles' base camp. This nocturnal walking about was no aimless journey. Archie was returning to the site of the day's battle.

This was a one-man patrol with the dangerous mission of penetrating enemy territory and not only searching out a suspected communications complex, but going inside for a look around. This assignment was Falconi's idea. Now that he had the army's craftiest scout back in the detachment fold, the colonel damned well planned on taking advantage of the guy's talents.

The intrepid Black Eagle scout was stripped down for this dangerous undertaking. He wore a black scarf pirate-fashion over his head to keep his hair from being entangled in brush or tree limbs. To keep the flesh of his face from being visible or reflecting light, Archie, using his fingers, had streaked his face, neck, and hands with black camouflage coloring. Another ploy for invisibility was his darkly patterned tiger fatigues. He also kept his uniform tied down around his wrists and ankles, and the pockets were empty so there would be nothing to make noise.

Archie carried two weapons with him. One was a .45 automatic pistol with three extra magazines, the other a fixed-blade knife that sported six inches of cold, sharp steel. This limited but effective weaponry was carried inside the jacket on a double-shoulder harness that kept the lethal killing tools out of the way of foreign objects that might catch on them were they toted in the conventional manner on a pistol belt.

Archie had also left his dogtags behind because of the tendency for them to jangle even if they were covered with plastic. As a final test of his ability to move as silently as possible, he had stood in front of Lt. Col. Robert Falconi and Sgt. Major Top Gordon. Archie had jumped up and down numerous times until the two veteran jungle fighters were certain there was no jingling or other unnecessary sounds.

The final ordeal before actually departing on the patrol was for Archie to crawl inside a light-proof hootch for an hour. This crude device was made with a framework of limbs overlaid with ponchos and palm fronds until it was pitch-dark inside. This allowed Archie's "visual purple," the stuff around the insides of the eyeball, to become activated. This was what the human system used when it was necessary to see as clearly as possible at night. By glancing slightly sideways at objects he wished to view, Archie would be able to pick them out much clearer. This actually took quite a bit of practice, but Archie had done it hundreds of times in the past, and was an expert in this particular technique. The main drawback with this was that any sort of brightness would destroy that visual purple in an instant. But it was a valuable enough natural commodity to utilize as long as possible.

When Archie left the hootch to begin his patrol, the other Black Eagles were careful that no light, not even a match, would be visible to him. It was probable that he would eventually have that built-up visual purple destroyed once he penetrated deep enough into enemy territory where the NVA would have illumination and vehicles traveling about, but in the meantime Archie would certainly have an edge over anyone else he might meet up with. During that initial entry into the badlands, the only glow he should have to worry about would be various types of rotted jungle wood that were phosphorescent and emitted a weak light.

Now, halfway down the hill toward his destination, Archie moved as if in slow motion. Each step and placement of his arms and hands was done in the anticipation of colliding with something. He constantly shifted his eyes back and forth as his sight drank in the darkness of the jungle and perceived trees and heavy brush in the way.

173

For more than two painstaking hours, Archie endured this ominous journey. A couple of times he was frightened into immediate stillness by a sudden noise. But several minutes of waiting had revealed the source of the disturbance to be some nocturnal creature on the prowl for food.

Archie knew, without a doubt, when he had reached the day's battlefield.

His boot crunched down on something solid and foreign in this natural environment. Archie slowly knelt down and meticulously slid his fingers under his boot. He felt something cold and metallic. He immediately recognized it as a piece of expanded brass left over from the shooting that had gone on that afternoon. He withdrew the object and slowly rolled it between his fingers to judge what sort it was. Within a couple of seconds, his sensitive fingers told him that it had been fired from an M16. It might have been one of those that the automatic riflemen Paulo Garcia, Malpractice McCorckel, or Hank Valverde had spewed out at the charging NVA. Or it might have even been one of his own.

Archie delicately laid the spent cartridge back on the ground and continued forward. It took him ten minutes to travel forward as many meters before he stopped again.

There was a sound—barely discernible—in the gentle breeze that wafted through the trees.

Archie, every hearing nerve in his ears strained to send any perception, no matter how faint, to the brain, listened intently.

At first there was nothing. After five minutes the scout began to think he'd imagined the sensation.

Then suddenly it was there again—a muffled, alien sound that did not fit into the natural environment of the jungle:

A human voice.

After another quarter of an hour Archie knew what direction it came from. It was exactly between himself and the area he had picked as the most likely site of the communications complex. The Black Eagle scout moved obliquely, picking a direction that would carry him past the point.

Now he crawled.

Archie reached out ahead of him on this unseen route making sure there was nothing on the ground that would cause any noise should he put his knee on it. He put his fingers out and gently lay down the tips with the delicacy of an operating surgeon. He touched something leathery that suddenly moved. Cold fear gripped Archie as he instinctively withdrew his hand.

The sudden rustle and hissing gave away the cobra's position. The snake was even better adapted to the dark than Archie. The reptile didn't need any visual purple, it had its heat-sensing tongue that told it the exact location of the big human in its proximity.

Archie pulled back and sensed the movement to his front. The serpent had struck and would make another attempt. Ferocious and territorial, it sensed the helplessness of the man. But Archie, unlike the cobra, didn't operate on instinct. He had intelligence—added to the fact that Archie could be as mean as any damned snake when he was pissed off—and Archie went to the ground to look up toward the lighter sky that showed through the trees. The hooded reptile moved, but this time could be seen.

Archie's knife slashed at the right moment, its razor-sharp edge going deep into the serpent. The scout quickly withdrew as the cobra writhed and now struck out blindly. The wound was mortal and disabling, and the snake rolled and twisted off to one side. Archie, damning silence, got to his feet and risked a dozen quick steps out of the area before sinking down again.

Another ten minutes of listening only revealed the weakening struggle of the dying cobra, until even that ceased. Ten minutes later the Red soldiers in the vicinity could easily be heard speaking softly to each other. Archie silently sneered at this lack of noise discipline on their part before continuing the patrol.

He moved on past the NVA outpost and turned back to his original track. When his sense of direction showed he was in the right place, Archie continued down the hill.

After an hour Archie's visual purple was blown to hell by the headlights of the Soviet army truck on the road twenty meters ahead. This was the exact spot that he figured would lead him to the target area.

The going was easier now. He could follow the road while remaining just inside the tree line. Other vehicles passed by on three separate occasions, but each time the noise and light alerted the infiltrator. Finally he reached a bend in the road and came to a complete stop.

There was an inexplicable guard post in the road. It seemed pointless to have one there. The strange situation warranted a thorough investigation. Archie settled down to check things out.

He didn't have long to wait. Another truck appeared and approached the guards. It slowed down to about a mile an hour. Archie could see the guards in the headlights rush to two sides of the road. They pulled on some ropes and a cleverly constructed camouflaged netting that was nearly invisible suddenly parted, showing the entrance into a large open area in what had seemed to be solid jungle only moments before.

Archie had found the complex!

Now all he had to do was get inside for a look-see. The Black Eagle moved closer to the road and eased himself under a frond bush at a point where the drivers of the vehicle had been slowing down. Again he went into a period of waiting, but this time there was no reason to keep every sense on a screaming alert. It would be a while before the moment would be right to attempt an entrance into the enemy area. In the meantime, Archie amused himself by daydreaming of Betty Lou. His mind tried to work out the problems they had in their relationship.

He hadn't solved a thing in the difficulties of his love life when the next truck came by a half hour later. Now Archie was tense again. He waited until the Soviet vehicle slowed down before dashing out behind it on the road. Archie knew that its bright headlights would keep him from being seen from the guard post.

It took less than a half-dozen rather frantic steps, and he was able to clamber over the tailgate and roll into the cargo in the back.

Archie struggled into the pile of burlap bales in the

truck. He rightly guessed they were filled with rice for the Vietnamese crew which worked on the communications site. He had just managed to hide himself when the vehicle braked to a stop. He could hear the exchange of words between the driver and the guards. Archie's knowledge of the language was limited to getting a drink or a piece of ass, but he did understand enough to realize that this talking was just an exchange of pleasantries.

The truck's clutch creaked, and the vehicle lurched forward to enter the bunker. Archie peered upward and soon realized that he was under an immense camouflage netting that was cleverly supported with a network of poles and cables. The Black Eagle caught a dim view of the moon overhead through the mesh as the truck stopped again.

The slamming of the door showed that the driver had arrived at his destination. Rather than get caught in the back, Archie slid over the side that led to the darkest area around. He softly hit the ground and withdrew deeper into the shadows. Now he was at a good vantage point and could clearly see the surroundings he was situated in.

The camouflage netting extended a full kilometer around the area. Directly in the center was an underground bunker that took up at least a third of the locality. He studied the structure intently and it took a few minutes for him to notice that a huge satellite dish was mounted on top of it. Strung with both natural and man-made concealment, it was virtually invisible unless the viewer knew exactly where it was. Archie surmised that more than one Black Eagle patrol had looked directly at the thing without even seeing it.

Not wanting to waste any more time, Archie took the pencil and pad from his breast pocket. Working quickly, he sketched the area, noting specific points such as doorways, guardposts, vehicle parks, and other features the knowledge of which would be useful to any potential infiltrators or demolition teams. Although this initial drawing was a bit crude, he would be able to improve it and elaborate the important details when he got back to the base camp.

Finally finished, he now turned his talents for observation to picking out a damned good escape route. Despite his unorthodox entrance hidden from view in the back of the truck, Archie was perfectly oriented. He knew which side of the complex he would need to leave from to be on the side where the base camp was located.

During the time he had spent spying on the complex, a crew of workers had unloaded the truck. The driver, evidently on a tight schedule, had immediately climbed into the cab and made a quick exit.

Archie had just begun his move when he was forced to stop by a trio of men leaving the bunker. He noted at first they appeared to be rather tall by Vietnamese standards. But, within moments, he could see they were Europeans. Archie crouched back in the shadows and let the three walk past him. They came so close that he could easily hear their speech. He caught one word that he instantly recognized. It was *zenshina*. Archie grinned to himself at the horny bastards. The word was Russian for "woman."

After the Soviets walked a distance on their way,

Archie slipped from the shadows and crossed the expanse of space to the other side of the netting.

He was forced to come to a quick halt. A slow, steady tread of footsteps announced the approach of a sentry. It would have been stupid to take the sleepy, bored soldier out with the knife. It would have meant having to either tote the body off into the jungle—a chore that had the possibility of being extremely noisy—or wait for him to pass.

Archie wisely waited.

When the time was right, he re-entered the jungle to renew his nocturnal journey. This time it would be back up the mountain to the Black Eagle base camp. A sense of dread suddenly flooded Archie's consciousness. The bad feeling wasn't from the realization that once more he had to tiptoe past NVA picket posts in the dark. Nor was it because of the fact that a slight slip or careless act on his part could bring down a whole troop of Red soldiers on him.

Archie's emotional disturbance was caused by something worse than even those problems.

The scout suddenly recalled that he still had to face a reckoning with Sgt. Major Top Gordon over his stint as an AWOL. And Archie Dobbs feared that more than the entire North Vietnamese Army.

waxed military auto that stood out so well from the other unkempt army trucks in the area.

"O-ye! Piss of a giant buffalo!" he cursed to himself as he cranked on the field telephone in a frenzy. The instrument was crudely mounted to one of the support poles of the sentry shack.

"A-lo," came the sleepy answer for the duty sergeant.

"Day Dai-Ta Drung," the sentry reported.

The sergeant's voice betrayed more than just a hint of panic. *"Chac-chan, Binh-Nhi?"* he asked.

"Of course I am certain, Comrade Sergeant. I cannot tarry, he quickly approaches." The soldier frantically hung up the phone knowing that the sergeant, wide-eyed and scared as hell, would seek out the company commander so that a proper greeting could be arranged for the regimental commander. The sentry covered his own ass by leaping out into the sun and properly presenting arms with his AK47. He braced himself for the inevitable confrontation with Col. Drung. Drung loved to stop at individual soldiers and grill the hell out of them with questions that ranged from nomenclature on the Kalashnikov assault rifle to quotations from Mao's Red Book.

But the colonel's vehicle, with several truckloads of troops behind it, shot right past him and roared into the garrison area before coming to a noisy, dusty stop. The sentry turned his head, then smiled with genuine sadistic pleasure as he saw the duty sergeant present himself with a stiff salute to the colonel, who had literally leaped from his command car.

Another officer appeared from the truck behind the colonel's conveyance. His shoulder boards showed that he too was of field rank. The way the men in the back of the other big lorries remained passive and silent indicated that they were a disciplined unit. There was no craning of necks to look around nor any unnecessary talking among them. They seemed a most serious bunch.

The sergeant, after executing another series of salutes, dashed off as Drung impatiently tapped his booted foot. The colonel turned to his companion. "You must remember, Comrade Major Ngoyn, that this is a rear-echelon guard company."

"Of course, Comrade Colonel," Ngoyn replied. He gestured toward the men in the trucks. "That is why my battalion is here, *co dung kong?*" The major's eyes swept the area with a critical gaze. He was not really too displeased. "The garrison is clean and orderly. That is a sign of discipline, Comrade Colonel."

"There is a veteran senior sergeant here," Col. Drung said. "He is an old sweat from the Viet Minh days by the name of Dinh. In fact, he fought near here in the Battle of Dien Bien Phu back in '54."

Ngoyn smiled. "I presume he tolerates no slackness nor inattention to duty."

"Correct," Dung said.

Their conversation was interrupted by the sight of both Capt. Truong and Sgt. Dinh following the duty sergeant back to the garrison area. Dinh limped rapidly and in great pain, but he managed to keep up with the other two for the short distance until they reached the colonel and major.

Truong stopped short and saluted. "Captain Truong reports to the comrade colonel."

Dung nodded his greeting and indicated the major. "Allow me to present Comrade Major Ngoyn. He and his troops have arrived most unexpectedly in the area. Because of this we much have an immediate conference with you."

"Of course, Comrade Colonel!" Truong snapped. "My headquarters is at your disposal."

As the three officers turned to walk up toward the building, Drung motioned to Dinh to follow. "This concerns you too, Comrade Sergeant."

Dinh quickly fell in step behind them. When they entered the crude office, Drung rightfully took the chair behind Truong's desk. "I understand you have had an engagement with the infiltrators," he said. "Please report, Comrade Captain."

Truong was embarrassed, but he knew better than to hesitate. He steeled himself and recited rapidly, "They penetrated several of our guard positions and we mounted an attack. I fear I must report we suffered more casualties than we inflicted." Then he quickly added, "But we are learning, Comrade Colonel! Believe me!"

Sergeant Dinh felt he must comment too. "I feel that under the circumstances, and with their limited experience, our soldiers performed acceptably."

Maj. Ngoyn almost sneered. "Only acceptably, Comrade Sergeant?"

"Yes, Comrade Major—acceptably," Dinh coldly replied.

"Never mind that," Col. Drung said. "That is now a matter of record and is of no consequence. I cannot waste a lot of time making judgments of comments on limited fire fights and other un-

184

important actions. There are two vital bits of information I must give you. First, we believe that intelligence has identified the infiltrators of this area."

"Who are the gangsters, Comrade Colonel?" Truong asked in anger.

"They are a special American group that has given us trouble in the past," Drung said. "I only know what higher echelon has passed down. But it seems they are particularly dangerous and it would greatly serve world Marxism if they were wiped out as quickly as possible."

"It shall be done, Comrade Colonel!" Truong shouted.

Drung smiled. "An admirable attitude, Comrade Captain."

Sgt. Dinh was more practical and didn't want to waste time voicing his defiance or determination to get the infiltrators. "You spoke of two bits of information, Comrade Colonel. What is the second?"

"It is good news, actually," Drung said. "Major Ngoyn and his troops have recently returned from active campaigning in the South where they scored many victories against the imperialist Americans and their running dogs of South Vietnam."

Ngoyn remained impassive. In reality, his outfit had been badly mauled on a couple of occasions and had managed only one minor victory over an isolated American artillery group unwisely posted on an exposed hillside.

Truong, however, was impressed by the colonel's words. "I congratulate you, Comrade Major!"

"Cam on ong," Major Ngoyn replied.

"The major's battalion had been sent north to rest

up after the arduous fighting, but the situation here has warranted that they go to the field to seek out the gangsters who roam the people's land," Colonel Drung said.

The expression on Truong's face displayed his disappointment. "I had hoped to have that honor," he said. "I feel I owe a debt to the great North Vietnamese people because of the previous setbacks which happened under my command."

"You will be allowed to participate in a limited manner, Comrade Captain," Drung said in a fatherly tone. "Do not worry. You will have your chance for glory in this affair."

"I am grateful for that, Comrade Colonel," he said sincerely.

"You and Sergeant Dinh may pick a handful of your ablest men to continue to search out and destroy the interlopers," Drung explained. "Major Ngoyn will assign you an area to operate in while he takes the greater part of the territory with his larger force."

Once again Sergeant Dinh had a practical question. "When you talked to us before, Comrade Colonel, you mentioned helicopter gunship support. Is that still available?"

"Yes, Comrade Sergeant," Drung replied. "There are three Soviet Hound helicopters at the air strip at Dien Bien Phu that will be available whenever Major Ngoyn calls for them."

"Then victory is assured now," Dinh said satisfied.

"There is one small situation that has arisen," Drung said. "And we must keep it in mind at all times during the operation."

"What is that, Comrade Colonel?" Truong asked.

"There will be some comrade tourists from the Soviet Union and Bulgaria arriving soon for a bus tour of the Dien Bien Phu battle site," Drung explained. "They must be allowed to enjoy their visit with the least possible interference on our part."

Maj. Ngoyn was not so concerned. "I am sure the enemy we seek is operating higher in the hills and deeper in the jungle than the tourist attraction. I seriously doubt if the comrade visitors' presence will affect our efforts in the slightest."

"Let us hope not," Drung said.

Dinh glanced out thew indow at the truck convoy of troops. "How many men have you brought along, Comrade Major?"

"My command now numbers some two hundred comrades," Ngoyn answered. "More than enough to accomplish the mission."

"I feel we may add another two dozen to that total," Dinh said.

Truong was offended. "More than that, Comrade Sergeant!" he protested. "Our men are completely dedicated to world socialism!"

Drung smiled in an accommodating manner. "Captain Truong is very enthusiastic in contrast to the quiet logic of Sergeant Dinh."

Maj. Ngoyn looked at the sergeant. "Why is your estimate of the number of your men willing or able to participate lower than your captain's?"

"Most of our men are not physically qualified for vigorous action in the field," Dinh explained. "But nevertheless, I think I can form an effective section from the company."

187

"Your candor is appreciated, Comrade Sergeant," Col. Drung said. He got out of the chair as a signal that the meeting was over. "I have instructed Major Ngoyn to contact you as soon as he is able to assign you to a sector. Prepare yourselves, Comrades. That is all!"

Truong and Dinh quickly saluted as the two field officers made a departure as abrupt as their arrival had been. Truong turned to his sergeant. "Quickly. Get the volunteers we need and prepare them immediately for the field."

"Yes, Comrade Captain," Dinh said. He went outside and blew his whistle several times. Within ten minutes the entire company had reported and was standing in correct formation.

"Comrades!" Dinh announced. "There has been a change in the campaign against the gangsters who prowl the people's land. We have learned they are a group of American imperialists who have come to rape and ravage."

The soldiers looked puzzled. Dinh had told them about that situation before. None were aware the Communist non-commissioned officer had not realized that what he had thought were lies actually contained a basic truth.

"We are now reinforced," Dinh continued. "Comrades from the fighting in the South have taken the brunt of the responsibility for this important mission. However, we shall still be allowed to participate in the glory in a limited fashion. Several of you will be allowed the honor and privilege of volunteering as a platoon of special shock troops."

There was a sort of unenthusiastic silence. The bad

188

results of the fighting they had experienced in their contacts with the infiltrators had smothered most of their combat ardor.

Dinh knew this, and he knew the proper way to react to it. He walked down to the ranks and began grabbing certain men and pulling them out of the formation. "You! A volunteer for the glory of the people! And you! And you!"

Within a short time, twenty very unhappy young soldiers stood out in front of their comrades. Dinh turned toward the headquarters building where Truong waited in the doorway.

"Comrade Captain!" the sergeant shouted. "These men have valiantly stepped forth to volunteer their lives for the glory of Chairman Ho's great revolution!"

There was a great deal of activity in the Satellite Communications Control Station in San Diego, California.

Some new software, recently prepared and loaded onto eight-inch floppy disks, had just come in to be used in an attempt to reboot SCARS—the Special Communications and Reporting Satellite—back to life. It was hoped this specially designed program would override the interference beamed at the orbiting device from Southeast Asia.

The technician slipped the diskette into the proper slot and turned to the keyboard to tape in the boot commands.

SCARS whirred and beeped—then died.

The engineer impatiently beckoned the technician

to step aside. He did some retyping and brought up the new booting program on the screen. He carefully scanned it to make sure it was correct. Then he tried the boot commands.

Nothing.

The senior engineer took over and repeated the drill. He removed the diskette. "A waste of time," he said sadly.

The technician took the diskette to put away. "Have they sent anybody into North Vietnam to do something about this?" he asked.

"That's not for us to know," the engineer said. "We can only hope."

The senior engineer stood up from the keyboard. "If SCARS isn't back into operation within three more days, we can kiss it good-bye. The thing wasn't supposed to spend any dormant time out there. Those circuits are going to stay closed if we can't open them."

"How will it affect the U.S.A.'s intelligence-gathering capabilities if it dies?" the technician asked.

"About like that iceberg affected the Titanic's ocean-crossing abilities," the senior engineer answered.

"You figure that's wroth dying for?" the technician wondered.

"There's some guys out there right now that think so," the engineer replied. "At least they've put their lives on the line for this thing."

The technician looked at the machine. "That's a hell of a thing to get croaked for, isn't it? All that's really involved is a bunch of wiring, circuit boards, and transistors."

"It's what it can do that's important," the engineer reminded him.

"Bullshit!" the technician argued. "It's the guys that might give their lives for this project who are important. Not a goddamned machine!"

"Oh, they're important all right," the engineer added. "And because of that they'll be getting plenty of attention from the whole goddamned Communist military establishment."

Chapter Eighteen

Archie Dobbs had quite an audience as he took the rough sketch maps he'd made in the communications complex and redrew them with more detail. The scout worked a with heavy concentration, but was disturbed a bit by Ray Swift Elk, who peered over his shoulder as he worked.

Finally Archie turned his head and looked up at the Sioux. "Do you mind—*sir?*"

Swift Elk grinned sheepishly. "Sorry." He went back and sat down between Top and Andrea Thuy.

"Great artists require concentration," Top said sarcastically.

Andrea, trying to keep the mood light, laughed. "It's not that, Top. The problem is their temperament."

"Let him work," Falconi urged his companion.

A half hour later, Archie was finished. He passed the sketches over to Lt. Col. Robert Falconi for the commander's perusal.

Andrea Thuy leaned over and gazed down at the drawings, and studied them. "Looks like we'll have to get our residential demo experts in here to decide the actual placement of the charges, huh?"

"Right," Falconi said. "Archie, go get Calvin and Blue."

"Yes, sir," Archie said. He got up with a nervous glance at Sgt. Major Top Gordon, who had been glowering at him during the entire time. "Anything you want, Top?"

"Sure," Top said. "Bring me a cold beer."

Archie smiled uneasily. "There ain't any cold suds around here, Top."

"Then there ain't nothing you can bring me," Top said as he exhibited a wicked grin. "We'll talk later."

"Uh, yeah, Top," Archie said. "I'll be looking forward to it." He quickly exited the area.

Falconi passed the map over to Swift Elk. "Archie did a hell of a job."

Swift Elk, now able to study the map without catching any crap from the scout, gave it a good looking over. "I'll say he did. Archie's really got an eye for detail."

"Jesus!" Andrea said. "You guys really make me sick!"

Falconi was surprised. "What's the matter with you?"

"When you three get together," she said pointing to Falconi, Top Gordon, and Ray Swift Elk, "you talk about how you've got to sock it to Archie for going AWOL. Yet when he goes out and not only risks his neck on a dangerous patrol but performs in a superlative manner, you don't say a thing about forgiving him."

Top growled. "*I* ain't forgiving him."

Falconi shrugged. "The sergeant major has spoken—that, my dear, is that."

Within a couple of minutes Archie returned with Calvin Culpepper and Blue Richards. Falconi invited the two demo experts to sit down. "Take a gander at this," he said handing them Archie's map. "And tell me what you think about blowing hell out of the place."

Calvin winked at Archie. "You found that damn commo center, didn't you?"

"I sure did," Archie said proudly.

"You're a helluva man!" Blue Richards said. He put his head close to Calvin's as they surveyed the layout of the target site. Blue looked up at Archie. "Tell us a little about it, Archie."

"It's a big area that's covered by a gigantic camouflage net," Archie began. "The thing must be half a kilometer wide. There's all kinds of support poles around to hold that covering up."

Swift Elk whistled in amazement. "That netting must weigh tons."

"Sure," Archie said. "It's built so well into the surrounding terrain that there's only one way for vehicles to get inside. They have to go past a guard point before driving up to the building."

"There's a building in the middle, huh?" Calvin asked. "What's it constructed of?"

"Concrete," Archie answered. "But I ain't sure of the dimensions. I saw the door open once, and I'd guess it'd run a couple yards thick."

"What do you think of the workmanship?" Blue asked.

"Sloppy," Archie answered. "I worked in construction in Boston a few summers, and I can tell you that the materials in that building are second-rate."

194

Blue looked over at Calvin. "Looks like a few two-and-half-pound blocks of C-4 ought to do the trick."

Calvin pointed to the drawing. "What's this thing you show on top o' the building, Archie?"

"It's a big dish antenna," Archie answered. "It looks like a heavy sonofabitch too. They got it held down with cables."

Calvin was satisfied with that. "Hell, if we breach them concrete walls, that thing'll help bring 'em down by its weight alone."

Falconi took back the map. "You two guys know everything you need now?"

"You bet, sir," Calvin said. "We can get our stuff ready now if you want."

"Go to it," Falconi ordered.

"Aye, aye, sir," Blue answered. He got to his feet and joined Calvin to go back to the detachment's supply of explosives.

Top, who had been scribbling in his notebook, said, "I got it all worked out now."

"Sound off, Sergeant Major," invited Falconi.

"Okay," Top said. "We leave here at dusk tomorrow—1800 hours to be exact. When we arrive here—" he pointed to a spot on the map he'd spread out on the ground, "the detachment will hole up and wait. That should be about 2300 hours. Archie, Calvin, and Blue can then continue on to the target and plant the explosives."

Andrea was getting very interested as she always did on the eve of some action. "Delay charges, I presume."

"Right," Top answered. "They should be set to go off at 0600 hours, the exact time the aircraft will arrive to pick us up and exfiltrate us the hell outta this operational area."

Swift Elk was stunned. "An aircraft? To pick us up?"

"Where, for God's sake?" Andrea asked.

Top smiled. "The colonel has already worked that out."

"Hell," Falconi said. "There's an airstrip down at Dien Bien Phu, isn't there?"

Andrea laughed. "What a great idea! The Reds have reconstructed the damned thing as a tourist site. It would add insult to injury to use it to escape after blowing up their damned communications station."

Archie was impressed too. "It sounds like a great way to wrap this thing up."

"It'll take a hell of a lot of exact timing," Top warned. He glared at Archie. "You heard my timetable." He checked his watch. "It looks like we've got thirty hours to go before meeting the aircraft. Think you can take Calvin and Blue into the target and out on that schedule?"

Archie rubbed his hands together. "A piece of cake."

"Okay," Falconi said. "Let's gather up the men and brief 'em. They might as well start getting ready now."

Top hadn't taken his eyes off Archie. "After that I want to have a word with you, sport."

Archie swallowed hard. "Yes, Sergeant Major!"

The gate at the entrance of the communications site had been torn down and pushed to one side.

This drastic action was necessary to allow the admittance of the troops and equipment belonging to Maj. Ngoyn's battalion. The unit, though only two-hundred strong, was in tip-top combat condition in more ways than one.

All were proven veterans of the fighting down south. The experience they'd gone through down there had made them battle-wise and cool in this unexpected operation they'd been thrown into by their superior officers.

The battalion's logistical situation was first-rate. All their worn gear had been turned in for better equipment as part of the routine that relieved units went through when brought back up north.

Even the small detachment from the guard company commanded by Captain Truong and Sergeant Dinh was in damned good shape. The weaponry and field gear they sported were hardly used because their primary duties involved keeping watch over a village of miserable peasants. Well-fed and in reasonably good physical condition, these twenty men could add quite a bit to the effort that Maj. Ngoyn's battalion was going to expend in this operation.

The Russian technicians manning the complex communications equipment inside the concrete structure left the comfort of the air-conditioned interior to come outside and watch the frantic activity that was going on around the area.

A network of earthen fighting positions was the first order of business. Dirt flew as a couple of hundred spades dug into the soft earth. Within two solid hours of unrelenting labor, there was a complex of fighting positions that were connected by communication trenches and field-telephone wire. The work went on steadily until the sound of distant helicopter engines could be heard.

Ngoyn's men instinctively froze. Several dove to the ground. The major cursed and shouted out at them. "Fools! You do not have to fear those aircraft. They are not American. These are the Soviet Hound helicopters you have been told about. *Durng len!* Get back to work."

Embarrassed and grinning sheepishly at each other, the soldiers resumed their laboring. Down in South Vietnam, the arrival of such flying machines always meant that American raiders had come into their area. It was bad news.

After another hour of digging, the place was well-prepared for any sort of attack. Squads were assigned their sectors and they all immediately settled in to follow the soldierly custom of making one's new environment as comfortable as possible.

Capt. Truong wisely let Sgt. Dinh organize their own small sector. The veteran non-commissioned officer personally inspected each man's firing position and saw to it that grenade sumps were dug. These holes, actually miniature tunnels dug into the slanted floors, would serve as a natural channel for any grenades tossed into the trench. Hopefully, the explosive devices would go into those tunnels and detonate harmlessly in the dirt under the soldiers' feet.

The Russians, who had been watching all this, grew terribly uncomfortable in the steamy heat. Now thoroughly miserable and soaked in sweat, they returned to their own area. Noise and light discipline were put into immediate effect as the front gate was returned to its original state. From all appearances, the communications site was the same as it always been since its construction. The new trenches were practically invisible until the observer was almost on top of them.

Next, Maj. Ngoyn followed his own personal philosophy about the proper way to conduct war. He began sending out squads of men in a vigorous program of patrol activities.

One of the first ones was a section from the guard company led by Capt. Truong. The young officer was most anxious to find the glory of battle that had so cruelly eluded him before in his military career.

Archie Dobbs walked slowly across the expanse of the base camp. He strolled with the greatest reluctance as he gradually approached Sgt. Major Top Gordon's hootch. When he arrived, he spoke out softly. "Top?"

Top Gordon crawled out of his primitive quarters and stood up. "What took you so long?"

Archie smiled apologetically. "I had to get my stuff ready for tomorrow."

"Let's take a stroll, Dobbs," Top said. The two walked out of the camp and into the jungle for several meters. When they stopped, Top spoke calmly and with great control. "You damned near let us down."

"I know," Archie said. "If it's any consolation to you, Top, I felt like hell when I learned from Fagin you guys was committed. I mean it, Sergeant Major.

I never felt so bad in my life."

"Dobbs, when you go to town and get drunk, it ain't so bad," Top said. "Or coming back late for reveille in garrison ain't serious neither. Hell, we expect guys in an outfit like ours to do more than just bend the rules. But you did the worst thing a soldier can do. You know what that is, don't you?"

"Sure," Archie said. "I missed a troop movement."

"That's exactly what you did," Top said. "They've shot guys for that. It's a grave offense."

"But, Jesus, Top!" Archie said feeling defensive. "If you'd given me permission to go to Saigon I still wouldn't've been at Nui Dep when Fagin showed up."

"Even if you hadn't been in garrison at the time, we could have fetched you in if you'd been on a pass. As it was, we really didn't have a chance to get ahold of you. Nobody had the slightest idea where you might have been. Long Binh? A local lockup? Laying knifed in a Saigon alley? Who could have figured it out?"

"Well, hell, I had to keep a low profile on account o' the MPs," Archie said.

"It don't matter why, Dobbs," Top said. He paused almost as if he were reluctant to continue. But he had to do his job. "I ain't letting this slip by."

"I know, Sergeant Major."

"All the guys in the Black Eagles have a job," Top said. "Even if it's only to tote bullets for a machine gun like Tiny Burke. But a job is a job, and when the guy ain't there to pull his weight, the whole unit suffers."

"I was wrong," Archie said. "I ain't arguing that."

"When are you gonna wise up?" Top asked.

"You're getting too old for this happy horseshit game you keep playing. You're a professional private, Dobbs. And this here modern army is running out of places for that kind o' guy. This here war in Vietnam is gonna end some day. Then what're you gonna do? Go back to the peacetime Army and fuck up so bad in garrison that they give you a general discharge? Is that what you want, Dobbs?"

"Hell, no," Archie said.

"That's what's gonna happen some day if you don't straighten up your act," Top said. "And like I said—I ain't letting this last fuckup slide by. I'll deal with it after the mission."

"Okay, Sergeant Major."

"Get on back to your hootch and finish squaring away your gear," Top said.

"Right," Archie said. He felt miserable. Deep in his heart he wished Top Gordon would kick the hell out of him. But he knew that the sergeant major's anger was cold and calculated.

Top watched the malefactor walk away. Then he checked his watch.

Twenty-eight hours until the arrival of the plane.

Chapter Nineteen

It was 1800 hours, with twelve hours to go for the rendezvous with the escape aircraft.

The Black Eagles had made a total commitment to the concept of this final phase of the operation.

Sparks Johnson's final transmission back to SOG Headquarters at Peterson Field was now history. His message had been in code and necessarily quite simple:

Will meet aircraft 0600 hours
airfield coord 1032502150

After that the radio was taken apart and smashed before being buried deep in the soft soil twenty meters outside the base camp. Archie Dobbs, as the recipient of Sgt. Major Gordon's ire, was detailed to perform the honors. Shirtless, he swung his entrenching tool until a hole six feet wide by six feet long by six feet deep had been dug. Then he climbed out and kicked the bits of communications gear into the minor crater that had taken him more than two hours to create.

The sergeant major, as dour as ever, watched the proceedings with an impassive expression on his rugged face. He lit a cigar, then spat. "Fill it in, Dobbs."

"Yes, Sergeant Major," Archie said. "Remember when you first came to the unit and made me do this?"

"Yeah," Top responded.

Archie grinned. "Well, it ain't getting any easier, Top."

"I didn't expect it would," Top said. "Hustle it up!"

Archie set about the task, made doubly hard in the steamy heat, scraping the loose dirt back into the excavation. When he finished he turned to face Top. "I don't want to sound a negative note here, but that radio ain't gonna be worth a damn to nobody anymore."

"That's the idea of busting it up and burying it, Dobbs," Top said. "If the NVA happen on this base camp and nose around here, they might find where this hole was dug. They might even dig down to see what we buried here. If they do, all they'll find is junk."

"Good idea," Archie said. "But that big radio was the only commo gear we had that could talk to Saigon. Them Prick-Six radios are just for jabbering amongst ourselves. We're kinda cut off, ain't we?"

"We're on our lonesome, all right," agreed Top. "Kinda makes you hope that airplane that's coming to pick us up arrives at the right spot at the right time, don't it?"

"Oh, it do! Yes, it do!" Archie said.

"Get back to your gear and get ready to move out," Top said checking his watch. "It's just about zero hour."

When Falconi had said he wanted to head for the target area at 1800 hours, he wasn't kidding. He watched the sweep hand on his watch ease up to the 12. When it arrived, and only then, he notioned to the detachment that was loaded up for the trek. "Let's go!"

Archie, up at the front in his usual position as scout and point man, waved back at his commander. *Calcitra clunis,* he responded. He turned and moved out with the rest of the Black Eagles behind him.

The going was even slower than when Archie had gone out on his solo patrol. One man moving had to be careful enough about noise discipline. But when seventeen people were involved, they had to be doubly concerned about making a racket.

Archie, in choosing the trail, made sure there was no place that might be eroded away by numerous boots. That could cause falls, or just plain make the going that much rougher. He also avoided tangled areas and places with a lot of deadfall for the very same reason.

Everything was routine for an hour and a half. Detachment communications, when necessary, was either handled with arm-and-hand signals or by speaking in low tones into the mouthpieces of the Prick-Six radios. Archie called frequent halts so he could move forward and make some careful observations before he returned to contact his charges to renew their journey. All the standard procedures for area security were practiced. Back in Calvin's Crapshooters—the last team in the column—Doc Robichaux covered the rear by constantly turning around and making quick but efficient eye-scans for any interlopers that might try to sneak up on them.

But they still ran into the NVA patrol toward dusk.

Archie sighted the green-uniformed Red soldier when the man was five meters away approaching from the opposite direction. Both of them were skilled veterans and moving silently through the jungle. Archie and his opponent responded with several quick shots that sent both 5.56- and 7.62-millimeter slugs slapping harmlessly through the air.

Within only seconds a quick battle developed in the tropical glen. The din of shooting built up as both sides began maneuvering for position while trying to feel each other out at the same time.

Lt. Col. Robert Falconi, however, had other things on his mind. He wanted to break contact and somehow sneak around the enemy. A movement like this was vital as hell to his plans.

The time was 1930 hours, and there were ten and a half hours to go before the aircraft would land at the airstrip on Dien Bien Phu.

"Eagle Two!" Falconi said into his radio to Top Gordon. "Move to the right and try a flanking movement. If you make it, settle down to hold for a while!"

Andrea Thuy, sending sweeps of flying bullets over the heads of Ray's Roughnecks to the front, rightly figured out the commander's tactics. "Is Top going to anchor himself down so we can use his guys as a pivot to swing around on?"

"Right," Falconi replied. "If he pulls it off, he can cover any movement in that area without a problem."

Top, for his part, didn't know anything about the tactical scheme of the situation. As far as the old soldier was concerned, he'd received orders to move to the right and try a flanking movement. "Move to the right of Ray's team!" he yelled over the fusillades sweeping back and forth. "Then get down to provide covering fire!"

Salty O'Rourke and Malpractice McCorckel led the way. Blue Richards covered the right and Top took the left as they moved through the heavy brush.

A couple of NVA had detached themselves from their buddies on an independent maneuver of their own. Being veterans, they had pulled it off pretty good by going wide around Ray's Roughnecks in the front. They also made a good tactical decision when they chose their point to turn in and rush the Americans. Unfortunately for them, they stumbled into the middle of Top's Terrors doing exactly the same thing from an opposite direction.

Blue caught a quick glimpse of their bright green clothing. There was no time for fancy shooting. He simply pumped the trigger in an effort to throw them off the track.

Surprised and angry at this unexpected development, the two moved to their right and stumbled onto both Salty and Malpractice. A brief exchange of shots followed and it was over at almost the same time it begun.

The two NVA crumpled and fell under the double salvos from the Black Eagles, who had to leap over the twitching bodies as they moved into their newly assigned positions. Top, closing in, found the enemy duo. He paused long enough to blow some extra shots into them to make sure they wouldn't be rolling over and trying some extracurricular firing into his men's backs.

"Hold up!" Top ordered. He pulled his radio up to his sweating face. "Eagle, this is Eagle Two. We're in position. Over."

"Roger," Falconi said. He now had Archie, Sparks, and Andrea with him. Gunnar Olson and Tiny Burke had moved backward under his instructions to provide the extra firepower from their M60 machine gun where and when needed.

"Eagle One, Eagle Three," Falconi transmitted almost frantically. "Move to our right. I say again! Break contact, and move to our right!"

Neither Ray nor Calvin made any reply under the circumstances. They simply didn't have time. A few terse words, and both the Roughnecks and Crapshooters pulled back, then hauled ass to the new positions.

Finally they were all well-situated. There was a bit of bumping between the flankers, but both fire teams ended up in the right place.

The NVA patrol commander tried a couple of probes to feel out the fluid situation, but all it got him were four of his men blown away in a hail of

Black Eagle bullets.

Now Gunnar and Tiny had situated themselves on higher ground a few scant meters behind Top's team, which anchored the line. Gunnar, a cool professional, blasted grazing fire out to the front, sending leaves, limbs, and dust swirling through the air as the heavy slugs slammed into the target area.

Andrea, providing security for the machine-gun team, now did little shooting as she made sure no individuals or groups of NVA broke through to charge them. Archie, backing her up, also held his rate of fire down.

Falconi also was not actively fighting anymore. He took quick radio reports from his three team leaders to get an assessment of the situation. It looked good. Now was the time for the whole Black Eagle detachment to break contact and pull back before renewing the drive toward the enemy communications center. He was about to issue the necessary orders when Calvin Culpepper's excited voice came over their air.

"Eagle, this is Eagle Three," Calvin said. "We got troubles. NVA reinforcements have moved up on our part of the line. Over."

"Eagle Three, what's your estimate of their strength?" Falconi asked. "Over."

"A whole damned platoon. Over."

Suddenly the battle's intensity soared. Continuous firing broke out on all sides of the line. Within five short minutes, it was the Black Eagles who were outflanked. The situation, which had only moments before showed every indication of working out to the Americans' advantage, now rapidly began to slip out of control.

208

Andrea crawled over to her former lover. "Robert," she said breathlessly. "We can't stay here much longer if we have to meet that airplane."

"To hell with the airplane," Falconi said. "Right now I'm concerned with getting out of this situation alive! If we manage that, *then* I'll worry about the goddamned aircraft!" He yelled at Archie and motioned him over. Then he spoke without regard to proper procedure into his radio. "Blue! Calvin! Report in to me. Now!"

It was 2015 hours—nine and three-quarter hours to the exfiltration.

Archie looked up as Blue and Calvin crashed through the trees and dove to the ground under a hail of enemy bullets, rolling up to him and Falconi. The lieutenant colonel, as he had been doing since the battle started, didn't waste words.

"We're pinned down here," he said. "The whole unit could never reach the target, but three men could."

"Us three, right, sir!" Archie asked unnecessarily.

"Right," Falconi said impatiently. "You got your demo, you know the objective, and you got the exact location of where the aircraft arrives to get us the hell out of here. Your orders are simple enough. Hit the commo station, blow it up! Forget timed charges. Make the thing go up as quick as you can. We'll use the cover to pull away from this place."

"Yes, sir," Calvin said. "We'll do it this new way."

"Afterward, go like hell to that airstrip. If the rest of us aren't there when the aircraft arrives, you get on it and leave."

"Hey, sir—" Calvin started to protest.

"Goddamnit!" Falconi snapped. "The orders are simple enough! *Get on that airplane and get the hell outta here!*"

The trio knew enough not to argue. Each instinctively reached out and clapped their commanding officer on the shoulder. Then they turned and left the impromptu command post to disappear into the thick jungle.

Andrea smiled grimly at him. "At least that will put us a bit ahead of schedule on destroying the target."

"Yeah," Falconi agreed. "But it won't help a bit in getting us out to the Dien Bien Phu airstrip."

AFter a bit more time had dragged by, darkness came quickly over the scene as the battle raged. Only this interference with sight and movement caused the fierce fighting to taper down to occasional shots. For two hours the Black Eagles endured occasional probes of their line. They fought off each in vicious, short skirmishes that died away leaving an eerie silence in the blackness of the jungle. Then the shit really hit the fan again as another small assault was launched.

This too was fought to a bloody standstill until an ominous quiet settled over the scene of combat. The silence, because all the animals in the locality had been frightened away, was complete as each side listened for signs of movement from the other.

Then this pseudo-peacefulness was broken by a nearby explosion.

The detonation rent the air with such a force that leaves were knocked from trees. A brilliant light made the sky seem as bright as day for a millisecond.

This instantaneous horror shocked both sides with both its suddenness and strength.

Andrea, close to Falconi in the dark, reached out and grasped his arm. "Archie, Calvin, and Blue made it!"

Falconi only nodded as he checked the luminous dials on his watch.

It was 2200 hours. Eight to go before their only escape from this hell arrived.

The engineer took the final drag on his cigarette and flipped it out into the parking area. He turned and went back into San Diego's Satellite Communications Control Station. When he reached the door leading inside the complex, he pulled off his identification badge and stuck it into the electronic slot. There was a short buzz and a click as the portal opened and allowed him to enter.

The engineer was a bit disgruntled. The job he was now doing would normally have been handled by a mere technician, but since SCARS—the Special Communications and Reporting Satellite—had been knocked out, he had been assigned the duty of monitoring its blank screen.

He went to his work station and sat down. The technician, now without much to do, sat next to it sipping a cup of coffee. The man smiled at the engineer. "Going through the drill again?"

"What the hell do you think I'm here for?" the engineer said angrily. "The goddamned chief thinks I got nothing better to do with my life than punch these frigging keys!"

"Jesus! What a grouch!" the technician replied. "Look, it's not my fault this situation has developed, okay?"

"Okay! Okay!" The engineer turned his attention to the cathode ray tube in front of him. He reached out and pressed the button. The system whirred and clicked.

SCARS leapt to life!

A white cursor streaked across the screen and the speaker emitted a series of signals that began to be immediately picked up by the main computer system.

"It's alive!" the engineer yelled. "SCARS is alive!"

There were some wild cheers from the word came on shift as they turned from their own assignments to view what seemed a minor miracle. Those that were able came to look at the electronic communications equipment that had been dormant for so long.

The excitement continued for another fifteen minutes before the others calmed down enough to remember that they had their own responsibilities to attend to. The engineer and technician both began the fine tuning necessary after the layoff forced on the equipment.

They were interrupted by the arrival of the chief engineer. He wasn't that excited when they jumped up to usher him over to SCARS.

"Relax," he said. "The crowd down earlier today from upper management. The program has lost its funds. Some guy in the Pentagon figured there had to be a better way." He reached down and hit the power button, turning it off. "And he was right. SCARS II will be installed next month, and it will be virtually interference-proof."

The CRT blinked, then faded back into nothingness.

"Gee," the technician said. "I wonder if anybody went to much trouble to get this thing turned back on."

Chapter Twenty

Falconi was hoping for more from the explosion than only destroying the Red communication center. He also hoped that another result of the big blast would be to unsettle and confuse the attacking NVA troops.

And he got his wish.

While the enemy soldiers glanced fearfully behind them toward the source of the monstrous detonation, Falconi radioed his attack orders:

"Eagle One, Two, and Three. This is Eagle. Mount a frontal attack." He turned back to Gunnar the Gunner and Tiny. "Give us all the support you can crank out!"

"You got it, sir!" Gunnar yelled to the commander.

The North Vietnam troops kept a steady barrage of pistol flares flying in the air. Although the light wasn't as bright as daylight, it provided enough illumination even in the deep jungle, to allow the men to see where they were going.

Gunnar the Gunner Olson, with the M60 slung over his muscular shoulders by a GP strap, moved forward with Tiny Burke beside him. He fired high over the heads of Top's Terrors, who occupied the center of the assault formation. Tiny, struggling along through the brush beside his "boss," made sure the ammo belts remained in an untangled state. The two, the strained expression on their showing the hard effort, looked alien and almost supernatural in the shadowy, yellow light of the Communist flares.

Up at the front, with Ray's Roughnecks on the right and Calvin's Crapshooters on the left, Top urged his men forward. Salty O'Rourke no longer acted as a rifleman. Instead he now employed his M203 40-millimeter grenade launcher to the front, firing out projectiles into the NVA lines. The other two grenadiers, Dwayne Simpson and Doc Robichaux, soon followed suit. A series of small blasts dotted the advance as the Black Eagles struggled forward through the rough terrain.

The initial result of the attack proved successful. The thin front line of the enemy unit was destroyed as grenades and heavy M60 rounds splattered into them. The NVA took heavy casualties and an unplanned, disorganized retreat resulted as the Black Eagles reached the advanced positions.

But the Red commander, Maj. Ngoyn, was an old campaigner. He hadn't played all his cards in this deadly game. He still held a couple of aces. It took him no more than ten minutes to deal out a counterattack in the form of strong reserves he'd held back.

Among these was the detachment from the guard

company under the command of Capt. Truong and Sgt. Dinh. The Communist attack was in the shape of a V with that unit at the very point of the farthest advance.

They ran straight into Top's Terrors.

One of Salty's grenades bounced off one tree, careened into another, then slammed into the ground between Truong's legs. The comrade captain took the hit in the lower belly as shrapnel stripped the skin from his thighs and disemboweled him in one terrible instant of blasting death.

Dinh, behind him, caught a couple of stray splinters in the upper chest and shoulders. Mortally wounded, but still alive, he managed to stagger forward a few more meters before he collapsed. The NCO went into shock, looking up into the flare light, but not really seeing his soldiers, who rushed past him in their battle frenzy.

A trio of these young stalwarts inadvertently walked into one of the Gunnar's salvos. The 7.62-millimeter NATO-caliber slugs chopped into them, knocking them to the ground like bowling pins. Those that came up behind them were more cautious, but they also dropped as Malcomb McCorckel and Blue Richards swept the area with systematic sweeps of M16 fire.

Thus, the detachment of young guards died, donating their lives to the Communist cause by soaking up a total of nearly seventy-five American bullets.

But the troops behind them were more than a mere reinforced squad. They were a company-strong unit of cagey veterans, who came in behind a screen of Kalashnikov bullets.

Top's men, being the farthest forward, were the first to slow down. But it wasn't long before Ray Swift Elk's and Calvin Culpepper's guys also were battled to a halt. The Black Eagles, with the Command Element now close behind them to lend support, made a superb effort at holding off this fresh attack. But, as the pressure mounted, Falconi was forced to be practical.

"All Eagles," he radioed reluctantly but quickly, "pull back to our original positions. Fire and maneuver!"

The retreat was short and orderly. Within ten minutes they were back in their earlier location, fighting off renewed assaults in the endless light of the flares.

Andrea Thuy, her beautiful face streaked by sweat and dirt, locked and loaded her M16. She fired full-auto fusillades across her direct front. A couple of battle-crazed NVA burst from the deeper jungle and attempted to cross a short, open space to find more cover. But Andrea's shooting slammed them to the ground. One rolled over a couple of times. The young Eurasian woman switched over to semi-auto and took careful aim. The bullet she fired hit the wounded man in the skull, sending a splatter of brains and blood across the bushes beside him as his head jerked under the impact of the slug.

Falconi glanced over at her. "You're taking this thing pretty personal, aren't you?"

"Shut up, Robert," Andrea said. She sighed another target and cut loose.

Falconi's radio, with the volume cranked up to high, came alive with Top's voice. "Eagle, this is

Eagle Two. They're pushing us in. I gotta move back to the Command Element."

"Roger, Eagle Two. Do your thing," Falconi said back. Two very disturbing thoughts jumped into his mind. If Sgt. Major Top Gordon said he was being "pushed in," that meant the pressure was at least ten to one. It also meant that when Top's Terrors pulled out of their portion of the line, Swift Elk, Calvin, and all their guys would be standing exposed without flank protection.

"All Eagles," Falconi said into the Prick-Six. "C'mon hone! Out."

Sparks Johnson now buddied up with Andrea. It was more than her good looks that attracted the Navy Seal petty officer. He sincerely liked the way the lady could shoot. The two, with Gunnar and Tiny covering them, providing damned good security as the rest of the detachment closed in on their position.

The din of battle built up as the Black Eagles crowded in closer. More Commie flares floated above the thick trees, and Falconi made a quick glance at his watch.

It was 0200 hours—four hours to go before the airplane arrived.

Maj. Ngoyn, with his headquarters staff moving along with him, eased forward through the thick brush. The NVA officer knew that this was a sure sign his men were pushing ahead and forcing the Americans back farther and farther as the battle progressed.

He yelled over at his adjutant. "Get a battle report from the company commanders! *Mau len!*"

The staff officer, utilizing a Soviet R-108 tactical radio being carried on the back of a nearby young soldier, spoke into the hand-held microphone. Within a few short moments he was able to report back to the battalion commander.

"Comrade Major! Both comrade captains relate that they are pressing relentlessly into the enemy lines. Resistance is stiff, but they are confident of victory by daylight."

Ngoyn, in a damned good mood, smiled at the adjutant. *"Tot!"* He looked at the sky that, even then, was growing lighter in the east. "Within an hour it will be daylight."

"Then we will no longer have to rely on the flares, Comrade Major!" the adjutant said.

"Better than that," Ngoyn said. "When it is light, we can call in the helicopter gunships!"

"Murng ong, Comrade Major! You will have a magnificent victory!" the adjutant shouted over the sound of the battle as they closed in on the fighting area.

Falconi had no choice. He had to pull back. The detachment was hopelessly outnumbered and there was no way that even the Black Eagles could smash back the growing attacks that slammed into their thin line of defense.

The lieutenant colonel called in his team leaders and gave his instructions for the retrograde movement. Andrea Thuy, squatting nearby, could plainly

219

hear the orders. She had spent her childhood in those mountains. Old memories had flooded her mind since her return, and she was nearly as perfectly oriented as Archie Dobbs was. This instinct included not only her exact location, but also any subsequent destinations any wandering might lead her to.

"Oh, Robert!" she exclaimed.

Falconi, irritated, looked her way. "What, Andrea?"

"I just thought I'd point out that that idea of yours is going to take us in the opposite direction from where we should be going," the woman said.

"What the hell are you talking about?" Falconi demanded.

"Well," Andrea said as diplomatically as she could, "you want to go *that* way, right?"

"Right," Falconi said.

"The only trouble is that Dien Bien Phu and that airstrip where we're schedule meet the aircraft is in the opposite direction," Andrea said.

Falconi spat. "Shit!"

By then the daylight had brightened the area until the NVA flares were no longer popping off overhead. Ray Swift Elk, now that light discipline was no longer necessary, fished into his pocket for a cigarette. He was just about to light it, but he stopped. "Uh oh!"

Andrea looked at him. "What's the matter?"

"Strain your ears," Swift Elk said. "You damn white folks can't hear as well as us Indians."

"I ain't white," Calvin said. "And I don't hear nothing."

"What the hell are you listening to, Swift Elk?"

220

Falconi asked.

"Choppers, sir," Swift Elk answered. "And they're closing in fast!"

A sudden, dynamic increase of incoming NVA fire caused the Black Eagles to hug the ground. Ricochets zinged in and out of their positions while solid slugs and tracer rounds blasted into tree trunks to send chunks of wood and bark flying through the air.

Sparks Johnson correctly surmised the situation. "They're forcing us down to let them choppers have an easier run at us!"

Roaring aircraft engines drowned out any further comments of the feisty Navy Seal. Then pure hell came to the jungle as six rockets—two each from three helicopters—slammed into the Black Eagle locality a pair at a time. That meant a half-dozen ear-crashing detonations that created enough concussion to cause several of the guys' ears to bleed.

Andrea Thuy wrapped her arms around her head and crouched in the thundering inferno. Falconi caught a glimpse of her and was tempted to crawl over to comfort the woman, but he fought down the instinct knowing it would do no good.

Tiny Burke, now bothering to do much more than duck his head a bit, looked up as the third and final chopper zoomed past. As the helicopters flew out to make a turn, the NVA infantry renewed their firing. Tiny looked back down at his buddy. "That ain't good, huh, Gunnar?"

"No, Tiny," Gunnar responded. "It ain't good. And we're gonna do something about it."

"Okay, Gunnar."

"Gimme a hand slipping the M60 into the fork o'

that tree," Gunnar said.

Tiny picked up the weapon and easily situated it into position. "That makes the gun point kinda up, don't it, Gunnar?"

"Yeah," Gunnar said, making a practice aim skyward through the now leafless branches of the trees around them. "We're going ack-ack, ol' buddy."

"What's ack-ack, Gunnar?" Tiny asked.

"Anti-aircraft," Gunnar answered. "We're up on a little hill, but them choppers still got to come in one at a time in order to fire their rockets and machine guns into this area." The Norwegian-American, an experienced helicopter gunner, understood exactly what the enemy air crews had to do. "I'm planning on us being a reception committee for them."

"You want I should wave at them, Gunnar?"

"No, hell no, goddamnit!" Gunnar said. "You just feed that damn ammo belt and kept it coming outta the bandolier nice and neat."

"Okay, Gunnar. I'll do real good."

Falconi had noticed the machine-gun crew setting up. He understood exactly what they planned to do. He crawled across the open space to join them. He checked the lay of the gun. "Looks pretty good, Gunnar," he said to the Minnesotan. "You think you can knock 'em down?"

"I'll do my best," Gunnnar promised.

"You'll have to do it fast," Falconi said. "We've only got an hour and a half left to get the hell out of here and meet that airplane."

Tiny hefted up a bandolier of the belted 7.62-millimeter ammo. "If we're late will they wait for us, sir?"

Falconi shook his head. "I'm afraid not, Tiny."

"Then don't worry," Tiny said. "Me and Gunnar's gonna get them damn ol' choppers."

"Save some ammo," Falconi said cheerlessly. "We've still got a lot of NVA infantry to break through after that."

Chapter Twenty-one

A dull, distant roar of aircraft engines was the first warning the Black Eagles received of the approaching enemy attack helicopters.

They barely heard this over the uneven staccato of shooting as the NVA troops laced the Americans' defense area with overlapping sprays of both full- and semi-automatic fire from assault rifles and machine guns.

The second warning was the sudden cessation of incoming rounds.

The Reds stopped shooting in order to avoid accidentally hitting their aircraft as the trio of choppers dove—one after the other—in a roaring aerial attack straight into the Black Eagle positions. When that happened, the sound of the motors was loud and ominous.

Gunnar the Gunner, anticipating the place where

the first helicopter would appear through the trees, properly aligned the sights of his M60. Tiny, tending the ammo beside him, craned his bull-like neck as he too tried to view the enemy.

The first aircraft, a big red star painted on its dull-green nose, sped toward them. Gunnar, one eye shut tight as he squinted with the other through the sights, gradually tightened his finger on the trigger. When the right moment arrived, he pulled it in a steady motion.

The M60 rocked-and-rolled in its position in the fork of the tree. Spent brass cases, reflecting the growing sunlight, spewed out and bounced off limbs and Tiny's big head as the tracer bullets streaked skyward. Gunnar had chosen this type of ammunition so he could track his aim better.

The sparking slugs arced slightly, then moved to the right in accordance with Gunnar's gentle manipulation of the weapon. He reached the correct aiming point, and the bullets slammed straight into the chopper.

The cockpit glass shattered and the helicopter suddenly veered crazily off to one side and continued on until it was out of sight.

"I got the pilot!" Gunnar yelled. *"Til lykke!"*

"You bet!" Tiny replied as he sensed the meaning behind the Norwegian words.

An ear-splitting explosion and a ball of red flame erupted a second later. Falconi waved over at his machine gunners. "Way to go, guys!"

But the second helicopter bore in before further congratulations could be offered.

Gunnar the Gunner gritted his teeth. *"Uff da!"* He

took another sight picture. *"Kom naerere!"* he urged the fast approaching NVA aviator.

This next attacker was a hell of a lot more aggressive than his buddy. No time was wasted in opening up with the aircraft's heavy machine gun. The atmosphere suddenly turned into a roaring, man-made storm of steel hail. The air seemed to crack with the heavy concussion as the trees around the Black Eagles split apart sending out stinging showers of splinters.

"Get him, Gunnar, for God's sake!" Falconi yelled into the thundering tempest. "The bastard will blow us off this hill if you don't!"

Gunnar's finger again tightened on the machine-gun trigger to send tracers hosing outward toward the helicopter. The Norwegian-American knew that he had only one chance to make his shots count. If he failed, the day, the battle, and their lives wouldn't be worth a fart in a windstorm.

The first bullets pinged off the chopper's nose with little sparks blinking across the metal skin. Then they dropped lower with Gunnar's aim until they hit the belly. A small but still impressive explosion blew out the bottom of the assault aircraft. It suddenly slowed and wheeled around in a lazy circular motion.

The third helicopter, charging up fast behind it, could not pull out of the way. It crashed full-speed into the other. The resulting detonation was so hot that the men on both sides gasped when they felt the heat.

Falconi didn't bother to ponder on the strange sensations of the incident. He immediately issued the orders he'd been wanting to give since the dawn's light first broke on that awful morning.

"Break contact! Pull back!" he yelled. "Haul ass, you bastards!" The Black Eagle knew the NVA would be momentarily stunned by the big crash, and he didn't want to waste a precious second.

The Command Element and three fire teams made their withdrawal with all the smoothness their battlefield expertise allowed. Even the veteran NVA squads on the front line did not grasp the fact that the enemy had melted away in front of them.

Andrea and Sparks, covering the machine-gun teams, waited while Gunnar pulled the gun free from the tree with Tiny's help. When the gunners were able to join the retreat, the two stuck close while keeping an eye out for any chance intruders.

Falconi led his men rearward as fast as they could move through the tangled jungle in front of them. Any elation he felt at the success of this retrograde movement was dashed by the thoughts of its temporary benefits, and the knowledge that they were moving farther and farther away from their rendezvous with the escape airplane.

It was 0530 hours. Only thirty minutes remained if they were to safely get the hell out of the operational area.

The retreat continued for another five minutes. Then it ended so quickly that the Black Eagles almost piled into each other.

Archie Dobbs, grinning like the cat who ate the canary, stood in a jungle clearing. "Hi, guys," he said cheerfully. "I been waiting for you."

Falconi, stunned with surprise, looked around. "Where the hell are Calvin and Blue?"

Chapter Twenty-two

Falconi, damning appearances, grabbed Andrea's hand as they and the others followed Archie through the jungle.

The colonel, his adrenalin pumping like crazy in the dangerous situation, felt an overpowering protective urge toward the woman he loved. Andrea, experiencing the same emotion, held on with loving gratitude.

They stumbled out of the tree line onto a hard-packed dirt road. The Black Eagle's initial shock at this discovery melted away at the sight of the big bus sitting there.

Calvin Culpepper, sitting in the driver's seat, leaned out the window and tipped his boonie hat to them. "All aboard!" he yelled. "Next stop Dien Bien Phu, folks! Now watch your steps, please!"

"What the hell's going on here?" Falconi demanded.

229

Top Gordon, joining up with the commander and Andrea, also peered around the area. "Yeah! What's happening? And where the hell is Blue?"

"He's on the other side o' the bus," Archie explained. "Guarding the passengers we put off."

The Black Eagles crossed the road and went around the big vehicle. Blue Richards calmly stood there with his rifle trained on thirty very unhappy civilians. All were Europeans, and about half were women and children. A very dejected North Vietnamese driver was in their midst.

"Bulgarian tourists," Blue explained. "They came here on a state-sponsored holiday to tour the Dien Bien Phu Battlefield."

Archie winked at Falconi. "They don't seem to mind loaning us their bus, though," he said. "At least they ain't voiced any objections."

Falconi let go of Andrea's hand and checked his watch. "Time is wasting. Let's go."

The detachment clambered aboard the bus. Calvin slipped it into gear and stomped on the accelerator.

Falconi looked out the back window and noted the obvious expressions of relief on the faces of the civilians as the armed men drove away from them. He went back to the front where Archie stood beside Calvin.

"Okay, Archie," Falconi said. "Fill me in."

"Yes, sir," Archie said. "After we blew up the commo station, the three of us hauled balls through the jungle. I figured we'd make a wide circle and go to the airstrip that way."

Blue Richards, seated in one of the front row seats,

chimed in. "That's right, Skipper. But we run into this here road. Ol' Archie noted they was fresh tar tracks runnin' up and down it."

"Tar tracks?" Falconi asked.

"Yes, sir," the Alabama sailor said. "You know, bus tars and truck tars."

"He means tires, sir," Archie said. "Anyhow, I could tell this was a well-used road. Naturally I made a comment on the fact."

Now Calvin, keeping his eye on the wheel, joined the conversation. "And I figgered you and the others was stuck up in that jungle and would be pushed away from the escape area instead of towards it. I read the tactical situation that way. There didn't seem to be much of a chance for y'all to bust through them NVA lines."

"Calvin's real smart," Blue said. "An' he says, 'Hey, let's get a vehicle and wait for Falconi and the others to give 'em a ride.' "

"Yeah," Calvin said laughing. "We figgered we'd git a truck. We never thought a busload o' tourists would come rolling down here."

"They was easy to stop," Blue said. "We just held up our hands and the driver pulled right over. He didn't know what was going on."

Archie guffawed loudly. "The sonofabitch near shit his britches when he finally found out who he was."

Falconi noted the time. "Hit the accelerator, Calvin."

"*Calcitra clunis,* sir!" Calvin replied.

The bus picked up speed and soon arrived at a

macadam road. A sign helpfully gave them further directions by indicating that the tourist site of Dien Bien Phu was one kilometer to the left.

The bus roared down the road and approached the place the French had valiantly tried to defend so many years previously. There was a guide standing at the entrance. Obviously expecting the Bulgarian tourists, he displayed a wide smile as he waved a polite greeting.

The grin faded as the bus shot past the surprised man.

"Looky there!" Archie yelled, pointing out the front window at the faint spot in the sky. "She's coming in!"

Calvin instinctively leaned forward as he tried to coax more speed out of the lumbering vehicle. They bumped across the rebuilt French positions, finally careening out onto the air strip. He hit the brakes and came to a lurching, churning halt.

"This damn bus needs a good mechanic's TLC," he complained.

The aircraft, now fully visible, eased down on its approach. Falconi leaped out the open door and pressed the transmit button on his Prick-Six. "Mama, this is Eagle. Over."

The aircraft, its radio tuned to the crystal's frequency, quickly replied. "Eagle. This is Mama." He issued the challenge without wasting time. "What's Raggedy Andy got?"

"Cotton balls," Falconi answered. "C'mon in, Mama. We're gonna have the NVA on our asses in about ten more minutes."

"Say no more," the pilot said.

The airplane, a C-123, made a clumsy landing on the uneven dirt runway, then rolled toward the bus. It taxied over and made a turn before braking to a stop. The troop compartment door was flung open, and the crew chief, an Air Force staff sergeant, leaned out and motioned them join him as quickly as possible.

Falconi rushed to the airplane then turned to help lift the others aboard. Finally, after the last Black Eagle struggled through the door, the staff sergeant reached down and grabbed the colonel's hand hauling him inside.

"Thanks," Falconi said. He braced himself as the airplane began its takeoff roll.

The Air Force man closed the door and glanced out through the porthole. "You guys caught a bus down here?"

"We sure did," Falconi answered.

"Goddamn, sir!" the sergeant exclaimed. "The North Vietnamese Army must be getting awfully friendly!"

"Naw!" Falconi said. "The dirty bastards charged us double, then made us stand up all the way." He turned and walked down the double row of seats to find a place to sit down.

Andrea motioned him to settle down beside her. The aircraft slowly lifted off the ground and, rapidly gaining altitude, turned toward the south. Falconi checked his men, noting that he was going home with the full complement—plus two: Andrea and Archie. There hadn't been even one casualty.

Andrea impetuously leaned over and kissed his cheek. "How about a nice dinner in Saigon?"

"You bet, baby!" Falconi said. He glanced over at Archie, then looked at Andrea again. "Even if I have to go AWOL!"

Epilogue

The lieutenant colonel, a muscular KGB man named Gregori Krashchenko, labored up the steep slope of the rocky Russian mountain.

He carried eighty pounds of field gear strapped to his brawny body and gripped a Sokolov heavy machine gun in his meaty fists. The weapon added another fifty-five pounds to the entire load he carried as he struggled upward. His thigh muscles burned with the effort and the air he sucked into his suffering lungs felt as if it were coming from a blast furnace.

Behind him, struggling to keep up, thirty other men under similar circumstances each suffered their own private physical agony. They had begun the tortuous climb in a tight group, but were now strung out a bit. The strongest were moving ahead of the pack at a gradual but steady pace.

These men, all young and tough, were volunteers for a special mission. Their group had numbered a hundred at the outset of this demanding program, but the rugged curriculum and endless hours of preparation and training had finally whittled them down to these remaining thirty.

The candidates represented the cream of the Iron Curtain's elite forces. Their uniforms, though alike in that all were made of camouflaged-pattern material, differed slightly.

There were the green-and-tan splotches of the Soviet paratroops, the large brown-and-green blotches on gray preferred by Bulgarian mountain infantry, the green-and-brown spots on tan of Russian naval infantry, and other uniforms that included East German, Czechoslovakian, and Polish.

All the men had endured three solid months of brutal training in which bravery, physical endurance, and dedication were demanded of them. That special mission that they had all opted to go on was one that their leader, Lt. Col. Gregori Krashchenko, considered sacred.

A quarter of a way up the mountain in this, their final test, five of them collapsed. Broken in heart as well as body, these despondent failures knew they were out of the unit at that point. That left twenty-five to continue the struggle that could earn them a spot in Krashchenko's special detachment.

Three more gave it up at the halfway point. The other twenty-two, some now staggering from nearly unbearable pain and fatigue, approached the two-thirds mark, where two more went down from the torture.

Krashchenko turned and now ran backward as a display of his fantastic physical condition brought on by the iron-hard regimen to which he had submitted himself after accepting the challenge of commanding such a unit.

"Step out, you dolts!" he bellowed. "You mother's sons! Show me you're more steel than flesh and blood!"

Partly in anger, partly in fear, the candidates forced themselves to increase their efforts.

Fifteen more minutes found them near the top. But it was still too much for another four. One, coughing blood, went face down. Only a superhuman desire on his part allowed him to roll over and die looking up into the sun.

When Krashchenko reached the summit, he stopped to watch the others reel like drunken men toward him. Finally, gasping but managing to smile despite the pain their bodies felt, they joined the KGB officer.

Krashchenko looked at the sixteen survivors. He raised the machine gun over his head in triumph. "Congratulations, comrades!" he shouted in his guttural voice. "You have proven that your are the best of the best. Your physical courage and stamina have earned you the right to continue on this mission of honor for International Communism!"

Soaked in sweat, closer to tears, and now barely

able to move their cramping muscles, the volunteers managed to imitate their leader by pushing their own machine guns over their heads and emitting a cheer.

"In only a few weeks," Krashchenko exclaimed in a near frenzy, "you will be with me in Southeast Asia to hunt down and kill Robert Falconi and his Black Eagle gangsters!"

ASHES
by William W. Johnstone

OUT OF THE ASHES (1137, $3.50)

Ben Raines hadn't looked forward to the War, but he knew it was coming. After the balloons went up, Ben was one of the survivors, fighting his way across the country, searching for his family, and leading a band of new pioneers attempting to bring American OUT OF THE ASHES.

FIRE IN THE ASHES (1310, $3.50)

It's 1999 and the world as we know it no longer exists. Ben Raines, leader of the Resistance, must regroup his rebels and prep them for bloody guerrilla war. But are they ready to face an even fiercer foe—the human mutants threatening to overpower the world!

ANARCHY IN THE ASHES (1387, $3.50)

Out of the smoldering nuclear wreckage of World War III, Ben Raines has emerged as the strong leader the Resistance needs. When Sam Hartline, the mercenary, joins forces with an invading army of Russians, Ben and his people raise a bloody banner of defiance to defend earth's last bastion of freedom.

SMOKE FROM THE ASHES (2191, $3.50)

Swarming across America's Southern tier march the avenging soldiers of Libyan blood terrorist Khamsin. Lurking in the blackened ruins of once-great cities are the mutant Night People, crazed killers of all who dare enter their domain. Only Ben Raines, his son Buddy, and a handful of Ben's Rebel Army remain to strike a blow for the survival of America and the future of the free world!

ALONE IN THE ASHES (1721, $3.50)

In this hellish new world there are human animals and Ben Raines—famed soldier and survival expert—soon becomes their hunted prey. He desperately tries to stay one step ahead of death, but no one can survive ALONE IN THE ASHES.

THE SURVIVALIST SERIES
by Jerry Ahern